In the manse that perched upon the high rocks like a mountain goat, the Harskeel regarded itself in a floor-to-ceiling mirror, feeling for the first time in years a real sense of hope. That barbarian along the high road—could he be the one? Surely he was brave—he had faced six-to-one odds. And the latest story, of how he had slain another in the village tavern, with no more effort or worry than a man slaughtering sheep—surely that added to his bravery?

The Harskeel in the mirror nodded. Aye, it seemed to say, the blooded sword of this one might well be the final key we have been awaiting for these last fifteen years. If this barbarian—named Conan, according to its spies—is the one, then we can be as we were before.

Yes. A pleasant thought.

Soon we shall have him, the Harskeel told itself. Already a score of our men prepare to ride. No matter how many must die, we *will* have that blade—and the blood of its bearer!

Certainly a pleasant thought.

CONAN

THE INDOMITABLE

The adventures of Conan
published by Tor Books

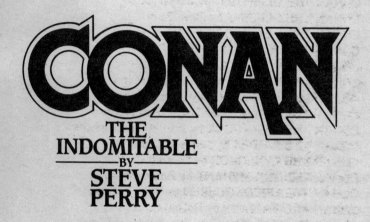

CONAN
THE INDOMITABLE
BY
STEVE PERRY

A TOM DOHERTY ASSOCIATES BOOK
NEW YORK

This is a work of fiction. All the characters and events portrayed in this book are fictional, and any resemblance to real people or events is purely coincidental.

CONAN THE INDOMITABLE

A TOR Book
Published by Tom Doherty Associates, Inc.
49 West 24 Street
New York, N.Y. 10010

Cover art by Kirk Reinert

ISBN: 0-812-50295-7   Can. ISBN: 0-812-50296-5

First edition: October 1989

Printed in the United States of America

0 9 8 7 6 5 4 3 2 1

For Dianne, naturally,
And for the boys and men: Rusty Medley, Steve Scates,
Greg Brown, and Slick Reaves, who would have helped
bury the body with no questions.

ACKNOWLEDGMENTS

There may be men who are islands, but I am not one of them; everything I have written has been a product of what I have done, where I have gone, and most important, who I have known. So it is with this novel. Mostly, the people who have helped know who they are, but I'll mention one in particular, since he made me a gift of the setting for this book during a late-night, wine-fueled discussion at his hilltop house in sunny Socal. Thanks to Michael Reaves, writer and sometime-collaborator, but chiefly friend. I owe you this one, Slick.

Hence, loathed Melancholy,
Of Cerberus and blackest Midnight born,
In Stygian cave forlorn,
'Mongst horrid shapes, and shrieks, and
sights unholy . . .

John Milton
L'Allegro

One

A man-high cairn marks the desolate juncture where the lands of Brythunia, Corinthia and Zamora come together. Centuries of wind and rain and snow and sun have worked their hot and cold hands and weathered claws over the pillar, smoothing it into little more than a soft-featured mound of stone rising from the barren ground. The mountain upon which the cairn squats is most always covered with snow, continually subjected to harsh storms, and it draws few visitors intent on seeing a geographical marker of such plain visage.

Upon the narrow snowbound path that passes the cairn walked a man and a woman. Arguing.

"There were horses," the woman said, "but naturally, it never occurred to you to fetch a pair."

1

The speaker of these words was named Elashi, a beautiful young woman born of the Khauranian desert. While lush of breast, she had the supple muscles and carriage developed by one familiar with hard work, and her legs were firm and slim from much walking. She wore a heavy cloak over a woolen shirt and long woolen skirt against the cold, and her feet were encased in high boots. A short, curved sword dangled from a strap at her left hip.

"Most of the horses were either dead or about to be," her companion said, his voice dry. "Riding a dead horse makes for slow going."

The man was also young, but certainly fully grown. He stood tall and wide-shouldered, with thickly muscled arms and a deep, heavy chest. Clean-shaven, he wore his black hair in a square-cut mane, and his blue eyes seemed to flash with a deep inner fire. Conan his name was, begotten of the fierce barbarian mountain people from the cold lands of Cimmeria far to the north. He too wore a woolen shirt and woolen pants under a winter's cloak and was shod in heavy boots, and the sheathed sword he carried was long and straight, of ancient blued iron, its edges sharped like razors.

"A lot you know," Elashi continued. "I sometimes wonder what, if anything, you are good for, you great barbarian lout!"

Conan shook his head. Since meeting Elashi at the temple of the Suddah Oblates, his life had certainly been less than dull. They had taken up with a beautiful zombie woman, fought a necromancer's blind priests and undead minions, and nearly been skewered a dozen times along the way.

He and Elashi had shared sleeping robes for much of the time, but despite that, she continued to harangue him at every opportunity. It seemed that she never tired of extolling his faults, real or imagined.

Conan said, "I heard no complaints last night as the fire dwindled." He grinned widely at her.

After a few seconds, and seemingly against her will, Elashi returned Conan's grin. "Well, I suppose you *do* sometimes rise to certain occasions." She was silent for half a dozen steps and then said, "But we would have more energy for such alliances had we horses to ride."

"I noticed no lack of energy on *my* part," Conan said. "And as long as we are wishing for that which we do not have, why not wish for a kingdom and servants? Or perhaps a palace of gold?"

"Oh, you, you—barbarian lout!"

He grinned again as she fell silent. After the death of Neg the Malefic, the necromancer whom Conan had slain, the young Cimmerian and Elashi had agreed to travel together until their paths parted. Conan intended to visit the wicked city of Shadizar, in Zamora, to ply the trade of thief, while Elashi's plans would take her farther south, to her native Khauran. From inquiries along the way thus far, Conan had learned that the route would not be direct; the best road detoured into Corinthia for perhaps several days' journey before looping southeast into Zamora again. Even as he recalled this, the path upon which they trod turned to the west and began to angle down the mountain.

Perhaps there was a village or town ahead in which he could practice his thievery and obtain enough silver for two horses, thereby putting an end to Elashi's constant carping. He certainly hoped it would be so.

Snow lay thick upon the land save for the path, where it had been trodden down. It was winter but clear, the blue skies sharp, the air cold and clean. Conan much enjoyed such places; towns offered much, but the air inside a city stank of odors unknown in the mountains. A man had to balance these things, of course. Meat and wine and lusty companions were more apt to be found in civilization than along a snow-covered trail in the middle of nowhere. While Conan's god Crom lived inside a mountain, he had never ordained that men were supposed to do the same.

From ahead on the trail there came a noise.

It was a small thing, the sound, and ears less sharp than Conan's would have dismissed it as perhaps a breeze-inspired shrub's rustling or a small rock dislodged by some tiny animal. The big Cimmerian stopped, and listened intently.

"What are you—?"

Conan waved Elashi to silence. When he spoke, his voice was a deep whisper. "Someone waits just ahead, around that large boulder."

Elashi glanced at the house-sized rock Conan had just indicated. "I see no sign of anyone," she said, matching his whisper.

"There was a noise," Conan insisted.

"I heard nothing. And I am a woman of the desert, do not forget."

How could he forget? She reminded him of it at least once daily. "Perhaps you need desert sand for your ears to work properly. I heard a cough."

That earned him a glare that, had it been a blade, would have left him in small and bloody chunks upon the snowy ground. "Listen, you barbarian oaf—"

"No more time for games," he cut her off. He drew his sword. "I sense that we are in danger."

Elashi nodded. Despite her verbal abuse of her companion, she had been with him long enough to understand that his senses were indeed sharper than those of ordinary men. She drew her own sword. "What should we do?"

"You circle behind the rock while I proceed along the trail to draw their attention. That way, you can take them unaware while they watch me."

"I will *not!*" she said, her whisper increasing in volume. "Just because I am a woman, you seek to shield me from risks! Never forget that I am firstborn."

Conan stared at her, amazed, as if she had suddenly sprouted wings and was preparing to leap up and fly into the heavens. He was young, and he supposed that he would learn more with age, but for the moment he did not think it possible that he would ever understand the motivations of women. Perhaps no man could. "Very well," he said. "*You* proceed down the trail while *I* circle behind the rock . . . and whoever it is that awaits there."

"Better," she said. But after a moment of triumph, her grin faded and she looked nervously at Conan. "You would actually send me along the trail into the jaws of possible death?" Her stare was incredulous and her voice quavered. She acted as if he had spat on her.

Conan shook his head and glanced around at the

mountains. Was there some demon hiding out there, sent to bedevil him? And what did Elashi want from him? Disagree with her and she argued. Agree with her and she argued even more. Crom! He felt the heat of anger rise within him.

Fighting to keep his voice level, he said, "All right. What is *your* suggestion?"

"Keep your voice down," she ordered.

Conan's anger increased as he stared helplessly at her. She was beautiful, to be sure, but maddening!

"You proceed down the path and draw the attention of whoever or whatever is there," she said. "I shall circle around the rock and get behind them. That way, I may take them unaware."

Conan stared, unable to speak in his frustrated rage.

"Isn't that a better plan than the one you had?" she asked sweetly. Warm goat butter would not have dissolved in her mouth, he thought. Surely, surely I have offended some god and this is my punishment. He stood silent for a moment, then stalked off without another word.

Whatever was on the other side of that boulder had better not be intent on causing him grief.

When he rounded the shelter of the rock, Conan found himself facing trouble. Five men stood before him; short, muscular, and swarthy, each held a dagger-tipped pike. They wore cracked and sweat-stained leather armor and gauntlets, and heavy boots. Behind these five a single being sat astride a tall black stallion. This creature wore a heavy riding cape, woolen shirt, and leather breeches, and held in a gauntleted hand a thin sword across the front of the horse's saddle.

Conan was somewhat puzzled about this last figure.

At first glance, it seemed a man from its dress and manner; on closer examination, the beardless face was definitely female, this self-evident not merely from its smoothness of complexion but from its shape and the bearer's use of cosmetics. The lips were rouged, the eyebrows partially plucked, and the area around the eyes darkened with a bluish hue. The reddish-brown hair was shorter than Conan's own, and cut feathery on the ends. Additionally, the creature's shirt front jutted out in twin peaks that certainly seemed womanly . . . but the crotch of the tight leather breeches revealed a bulge than seemed most definitely male.

Conan's examination of the horsed figure was interrupted by its speech. "Stand and deliver!" it said. The voice added to his confusion. It was deep, that of a strong man. Coming from those ruby lips, it sounded most odd indeed.

"Stand and deliver what?" Conan asked. "Are you blind, that I appear to be some fat merchant laden with gold or wares? What you see is all I own, and that is little enough."

"I will have your sword," the figure said.

At that moment Elashi appeared behind the six, clambering up the rock so that she was above them.

Conan swung the sword back and forth to limber his shoulder, then gripped the handle with both hands and aimed the point at the throat of the nearest pikeman, a techinque he had learned from the swordmaster of the Suddah Oblates. "I think not," he said.

The pikeman swallowed dryly.

"Do not be a fool," the horse rider said. "We are six to your one. Give us your sword and live. Refuse and die."

"I find it somewhat strange that you seem willing to lose at least some of your men to collect a sword. Such an exchange is bad business. I think that perhaps there is something else on your mind."

The man-woman laughed, a deep, throaty sound. "Wise, for a savage."

On the boulder, Elashi had put her sword down and was lifting a head-sized rock.

The leader of the bandits leaned forward on the horse. The creak of the saddle leather was loud in the otherwise quiet clearing. "Very well. Then we shall have to obtain that which we wish the hard way. Take him!"

Elashi chose this precise instant to hurl the rock she held. Now the desert woman was not much of a swordswoman, true, and she talked too much for Conan's taste, but apparently the throwing of rocks could be numbered among her skills: the large stone smacked into the head of one of the pikemen, felling him like a poleaxed pig. The sound of the rock striking the skull was much like that of a melon when smashed with a heavy board. That worthy would trouble no one else in this world.

Startled, the pikemen turned to espy this new threat. The rider's mount shied at the sudden movements, backing itself almost to the boulder. Before the rider could turn, Elashi, sword in hand, leaped upon him—or her—screaming.

Taking advantage of the confusion, Conan darted forward, swift for a man so large, and swung the ancient blue-iron blade. The stroke met flesh, cleaving muscle and bone, toppling a second pikeman into a fall that would ultimately end in the Gray Lands—and likely Gehanna.

Elashi and the rider fell from the horse. Conan had time to see the mysterious bandit leader leap up and twist about sharply; the movement spun Elashi away as a terrier tosses a rat. She hit the ground and rolled up, sword held ready.

No matter. Her distraction had accomplished its purpose. Conan swung his sword back and forth, chopping at the disorganized pikemen, who were at quarters too close to use their weapons effectively. Blue iron met pike wood and sheared it, continuing on to carve bloody canyons through leather armor. Conan's mighty arms drove the weapon he bore, gutting one man, removing another's head, driving all before the Cimmerian whirlwind. Before they could gather their wits, four of the five pikemen were down, one by Elashi's stone, the others by courtesy of Conan's blade.

The fifth pikeman deemed it wise to change occupations at that moment, to that of a fleet-footed messenger; he ran, dropping his pike to attain yet more speed. For an instant Conan considered retrieving one of the fallen pikes to use as a spear against the fleeing man, but decided that dealing with the leader was more important. As he turned, however, the rider managed to recapture the horse. Flinging itself onto the saddle, the leader of the bandits spurred the animal, which bolted straight at Conan.

The Cimmerian dodged, swiping at the rider, but the figure leaned away from the sword's arc and Conan cut nothing more than air. The force of the slash spun the young Cimmerian off balance. In a heartbeat, horse and rider were past, moving too swiftly for Conan to recover in time to give chase.

Conan watched the retreating figures of pike-man and rider. Came the rider's call: "I'll have your sword yet, barbarian!"

Conan shook his head. Why would anyone be willing to risk death for a sword of uncertain worth? In fact, while the blued-iron weapon was of good quality and quite serviceable, it had no intrinsic value. The handle was plain and leather-wrapped, not bejeweled or carved ivory, and the guard was merely a single bar of thick brass. The strange bandit leader must be mad.

Elashi approached, brushing dirt from her cloak.

"Are you injured?" Conan asked.

"Nay." She finished her cloak dusting and looked at Conan askance. "You let two of them escape."

He could not suppress a surprised grunt. "You never mentioned that you desert dwellers drank blood."

"Little point in leaving a job half accomplished," she said. "I suppose there's nothing to be done for it. Let us examine the corpses."

"Examine them? Why?"

She regarded him as she might a simpleminded child. "And you intend to become a thief? For valuables, of course."

Conan nodded at this. For once she had a point. But even as he rifled the sparse purses of the fallen bandits, the question of why they had attacked continued to plague him. And the man-woman's retreating threat to have his sword—what was that all about?

Well, he would pay it no more mind. It was finished and done with, and like as not, he had seen the last of that odd personage.

Two

Although the purses of the slain mountain bandits yielded only a few coppers, Conan was not the least averse to collecting the coins and sharing them equally with Elashi. Certainly the bandits had no further need for money where they were bound.

As the Cimmerian and the desert woman made their way down the mountain road, they saw in the distance a small village; thanks to the bandits, they could now buy food and a room for the night. Only a few days past, Conan had carried two silver coins, the last of his profit from the pelt of a dire-wolf he had slain. Unfortunately, as he had raced through the halls of the necromancer's castle, he had somehow dislodged the silver from his

12

purse. After the aggravation of the bandit's attack, providing supper and shelter was the least the dead men could do.

As evening sought to claim the day, stormy purple and gray clouds gathered on the horizon. The wind grew colder, carrying in its chilly teeth the promise of snow. Conan knew the signs: a blizzard was building. It would be most uncomfortable to be caught out in the open in the coming weather. The village lay less than an hour ahead by his reckoning, and the two of them should arrive there at about the time the storm did. If they hurried.

The village was like a dozen others Conan had seen in his travels. Perhaps a score of structures, most of them small houses of stone with sod roofing, sprawled along the sides of the road, now somewhat wider than it had been in the mountains. The largest of the buildings was, naturally, the village inn. The wordless sign over the doorway bore merely a carved picture of a sheep, doubtless detailing the mainstay of local industry. The building was also of stone, weathered and in disrepair, with oiled but torn lambskin over the windows, showing a fitful yellow glow from within.

As Conan and Elashi approached the inn, the snow began to flurry about them. In a moment the swirling winds had the powdery whiteness dancing thickly in the evening air. The combination of snow and gathering darkness quickly reduced visibility to a few spans.

"Not a very appealing place," Elashi observed.

"Our choices are somewhat limited," Conan said. "True."

He swung the heavy wooden door inward and took in the interior of the inn. The ceiling was low, hardly an arm's length taller than Conan himself, and the central room into which they stared was occupied by perhaps twenty people, most of them men. They sat at rude tables or stood near the large fireplace within which a fat log burned brightly. An archway at the end of the room led, Conan surmised, to sleeping rooms and storage for food and drink.

Stepping into the room, Conan shut the door behind Elashi, never taking his gaze from the occupants. Most of them were obviously locals: dark-complected, older men dressed in shepherd garb. There were a few women who matched the men in age and clothes, also likely local folk.

At the far end of the communal eating and drinking room sat a thin man dressed as though for summer in thigh-length trousers and a short tunic. He had hair the color of straw and a foolish grin upon his face. Likely drunk or slack-witted, Conan thought.

Behind this summery fool sat two men who looked very much like the five who had assaulted Conan upon the trail. There were no pikes in evidence, but each man wore a sword and long dagger ensheathed upon his belt, and their features looked hard in the light of guttering tapers mounted at odd intervals upon the stone walls.

Conan finished his scan of the room just as a tall and spindly man whose face seemed buried within the shroud of a gray beard approached. The innkeeper, no doubt.

"Ah, welcome, travelers. Would ye be desirin' food 'n' drink, then?"

Conan nodded. "Aye. And a room for the night."

Graybeard bobbed his head in an enthusiastic nod. "Done, done. Ye made it just in time, I warrant. 'Tis a howler startin' up out there." As if to punctuate his words, the wind whistled and blew a blast of snow through one of the torn shades. Graybeard said, "Lalo, cover that hole!"

The thin blond man stood and moved to the window, where he began to repair the window cover with a patch and string that he pulled from a pocket on his tunic. The man continued smiling all the while, and he hummed a strange little tune as he worked.

Conan and Elashi, meanwhile, moved to an empty table not far from the fire as Graybeard went to fetch wine and whatever passed for supper.

The meal, as it turned out, was not altogether bad. The meat was mutton, somewhat greasy, but edible. Hard brown bread accompanied the meat, and the wine was red and sharp but better than some that Conan had tasted. Elashi produced a small knife from her belt and sliced the meat into strips; Conan draped pieces of these over chunks of bread and washed them down with the wine. Certainly it bested foraging along the trail for roots and ground squirrels, as they had been doing for several days.

Graybeard accepted half a dozen coppers for the meal and asked another four for the room. Conan would have bargained but he was tired, and what did it matter anyway? The money had been his for only a few hours; he had not grown particularly attached to it. He paid for the meal and room, causing a smile to grow in the midst of Graybeard's hairy visage.

Over his third cup of wine, Conan began to feel somewhat relaxed. The journey along the mountains had been relatively uneventful—save for the inept bandits—but even so, it had been a long walk. With food and wine in his belly and shelter against the winter's rages, he felt most comfortable.

He should have known that meant trouble. Every time he felt at ease of late, something always seemed to come along to spoil it.

"Watch it, fool!"

Conan looked up from his warm feeling, to see the straw-haired man, the one Graybeard had called "Lalo," backing away from the table at which the two swordsmen sat. Apparently Lalo had jostled the table in passing and the occupants had taken umbrage at his clumsiness. One of the swordsmen was missing most of an ear. The other had a nose that had been broken more than once, and was decidedly bent to one side.

"Sorry, m'lord," Lalo said.

Bent Nose half-stood. "Are you making sport of me, fool? Calling me lord?"

"Why, no, m'lor—I mean, no, sir. 'Twould be hard to make sport of one such as yourself."

"That's better."

Lalo's grin never faltered. "I mean, there's so little to work with."

Bent Nose blinked, obviously not understanding.

At his table, Conan smiled. He might be called a barbarian for his looks, but he knew humor when he heard it.

Unfortunately for Lalo, One Ear's wits were at least a bit sharper than his companion's. "Fool," he said. "He has insulted you!"

Bent Nose looked at him quizzically. "What are you talking about?"

"Ah," Lalo said. "I see that you are indeed a wit." He paused for a second, then continued: "No, on second pass, I think that is probably only half-true."

Conan chuckled into his wine. Judging from Bent Nose's reaction, it seemed true enough.

"Why are you laughing?" Elashi asked. "Those two will cut that poor man into bloody ribbons!"

Conan shrugged. "That's his problem. A sharp tongue is no match for a sharp blade."

One Ear said, "Idiot! He insults you again."

This was enough for Bent Nose. He cleared his blade. "I shall have your laughing head for a soup bowl!" he bellowed, advancing slowly toward Lalo.

Elashi jumped to her feet, drawing her own sword.

Conan said, "What are you doing?"

"Since there are no *men* in here to protect a harmless, unarmed soul from such brutes, I shall do so myself!"

Conan sighed. Always something came to disturb his peace. He stood. "Be seated. I shall handle this."

"I would not want you to strain yourself," she said.

Conan merely shook his head. Is this a test, Crom? Perhaps I should have remained at the monastery with the late Cengh and given up women. They are certainly more trouble than they are worth, at times.

Bent Nose looked up to see Conan looming. He paused in his pursuit of Lalo. "What is your business here, outlander?"

Conan decided to try reason. "I have had a long day," he said, "and I would not see it ended by being blood-spattered. Why not allow Lalo here to live?"

Bent Nose shifted the point of his sword in Conan's direction. "I care less than mouse turd for how your day has gone. This fool insulted me and he shall pay for it!"

Conan, whose sword remained sheathed, spared a glance at Elashi, then at Lalo. "Perhaps," he told Lalo, "if you apologized to Bent Nose here, this matter could be resolved peacefully."

"Bent Nose? Who are you calling Bent Nose?"

Conan said, "Have you never used a looking glass?"

"I suspect the last one he gazed upon shattered when forced to reflect such a heinous image," Lalo observed.

"You help matters not at all," Conan told the grinning man.

"Yaahh!" With that exclamation, Bent Nose charged, sword uplifted to split Lalo like a stick of kindling.

Conan had plenty of time to draw his own weapon and block the attack, but as he pulled his sword free of the sheath, One Ear stood and threw his wine bottle at Conan's head.

While the Cimmerian's reflexes were fast, even

he could not slap the bottle from the air with the flat of his sword and then have sufficient time to block Bent Nose's strike at Lalo. As the glass bottle shattered against Conan's sword, Bent Nose's blade came down upon the hapless Lalo . . .

No! He missed! Lalo danced to one side, and the sword that would have cleaved him hit a thick table top instead, burying the blade to half its width in the wood. Bent Nose jerked on the handle, but the sword was stuck fast.

What Lalo did then was quite amazing. He danced back toward Bent Nose, grabbed his wrist and underwent some kind of contortion, twisting and turning as he dropped to his knees on the floor. Bent Nose screamed and flew over Lalo's head to dive face first into the nearest wall.

Conan had no more time to marvel over this maneuver, however, as One Ear charged, brandishing his sword and howling like a demented wolf. He sought to run Conan down, a mistake most costly. Conan merely extended his sword to arm's length and One Ear spitted himself on the point. Half of the sword's length emerged from the man's back, carrying upon its tip blood from his lanced heart. One Ear fell, and Conan managed to jerk his blade free as the man went down. He bent and wiped the gore from the iron on One Ear's tunic, not doubting for a moment that the man was dead.

So much for a peaceful evening by the fire.

Conan turned, to see Lalo and Elashi examining Bent Nose. From the angle of the downed man's head, it was clear that his neck was broken; and from his impact against the wall, likely his skull was broken as well.

Such proved to be the case. Elashi stood and said, "He is dead."

Conan moved toward Elashi and Lalo. Around them, the inn's other patrons sat frozen—so many figures in a painting—afraid to move.

"I have never seen that type of wrestling before," Conan said. "Very efficient."

Lalo's grin never wavered. "I learned it from the little yellow men of Khitai," he said. "I spent several years there. It is called jit-jit. By its use, a practiced small man may best a larger one, or even one armed."

"Interesting," Conan said. "Perhaps a man who tempered his mirth might not have to use it at all."

"Ah," Lalo said, "but you see, that is my curse." He paused to glance at the two dead men. "I appreciate your help, though I could have handled these two myself. Perhaps you will allow me to buy you a bottle of wine and explain?"

Conan glanced at Elashi, who nodded. Of course. And, he had to admit, he was more than a little curious himself.

"When I was a boy in the mountains of eastern Zamora," Lalo began, "my father ran afoul of the local wizard. A very subtle being, this wizard was. He could have caused my father's crops to fail or our cows to dry up, or perhaps visited a plague upon our family. But the magician was, as I have said, very subtle; and his magics were no less effective for this. He laid his geas upon the sons of my father."

Lalo paused to sip at his wine. His smile remained constant.

"My brothers—I had three—all perished from the effects of the wizard's curse within two years of its placement. In an effort to escape, I fled across the vast Eastern Desert to Khitai. To no avail, in that the curse stayed with me."

Elashi was leaning forward, fascinated. As for himself, Conan felt less interest now than dread. This tended to happen whenever the subject of magic was broached. Such unnatural doings were not to his taste. Still, the story was somewhat intriguing.

"It was there," Lalo continued, "in Khitai that I learned the fighting art of jit-jit. The Khitains are quite adept at such things. Eventually my curse caused me to leave there as well. I cannot stay in one place too long; even the most sympathetic souls cannot stand against the wizard's magic for more than a few weeks."

"What exactly is this curse?" Conan asked.

"I cannot stop smiling," Lalo replied. "And I cannot prevent myself from making sport of those around me. You, for instance, Conan, have so much muscle that it is doubtful you can stretch enough to scratch an itch on your backside."

"What?" Conan started to rise from his seat.

Elashi touched his forearm. "The curse, Conan."

Conan relaxed, understanding. "I take your meaning, Lalo."

The smiling man sighed. "Indeed. Imagine if you can what it would be like to be with a woman

and be unable to avoid insulting comments even
as you are joined together."

"How awful!" Elashi murmured.

"Here you have come to my aid against two of
the Harskeel's thugs, and even so, I cannot help
myself from haranguing you."

"Who exactly is this Harskeel?" Conan asked.

"Not 'who' precisely, but more of 'what,'" Lalo
said. "Its full name is Harskeel of Loplain, and it
is an hermaphrodite—half man, half woman."

Elashi inhaled sharply.

"You know of it?" Lalo asked.

"Aye," Conan answered. "We had an encounter
with it along the trail earlier this very day. Is it
perhaps mad?"

"Mad? What makes you ask, you apelike buffoon?"

Conan's anger stirred, but he forced it down.
The man was cursed, after all. "This Harskeel thing
lost five of its men in an attempt to steal nothing
more than my sword."

"Ah, I can see why you would think it crazed.
No, there is method in this madness. The Harskeel
of Loplain is also cursed, but by its own actions.
Once it was two separate people, a man and a
woman. These two were lovers, and desired more
intensity and closeness—not that a barbarian like
yourself could possibly understand such a thing—so
they stole a book of spells from a witch. Unfortunately for them, they bespoke the spell incorrectly.
It left them considerably closer than was their
intent."

"Ugh," Elashi said. "But what has that to do
with Conan's sword?"

"Actually, it collects swords from anyone who

shows the slightest sign of bravery. There is supposed to be a counterspell, some mantologic process that will return the Harskeel to its former state of two people. The spell involves the use of a sword dipped in the blood of its owner. If the owner is—or was—brave enough, it will trigger the magic. So far, more than a few men have died without providing the needed weapon."

"I thought this creature wished more than merely my sword," Conan said.

"Certainly it did not seek your brain," Lalo said. "Forgive me."

Conan merely nodded. He had heard worse from Elashi, and she was under no particular curse.

Lalo told them his time at the local inn was about up and that he would be leaving soon. Conan and Elashi also planned to leave as soon as the snowstorm ended, likely on the morrow. The three of them finished the bottle of wine and then parted, Lalo warning Conan to take care on his journey. Now that the outlander had slain so many of the Harskeel's men, the hermaphrodite would certainly consider him a candidate for the spell it needed.

As Conan and Elashi started for their room, she said, "A shame, to be cursed so."

"I notice he did not insult you during our conversation," Conan said.

"Why should he, when you made such a likely target?"

"The two of you would do well together," Conan said. "You have so much in common."

Elashi chose to be offended by this, which surprised Conan not at all. Hardly anything she did surprised him of late. When they arrived in their room, for instance, she lay against him under the inn's rough blanket, touching him and laughing softly . . . as if they had been newly wed that same morning. He shook his head, not understanding, but not minding this in the least.

Three

Deep in the twisted bowels of the Grotterium Negrotus, Katamay Rey once again called upon the slab of enchanted quartz. Under the dank-green fungal glow, the wizard scried, searching the depths of crystal stone for the future.

The clear rock became milky, then slowly cleared near one end, and the face of a man appeared. Strong featured, with black hair and fiery blue eyes, the man's face peered unseeingly back at Rey, unaware of being observed.

Rey made mystical passes over the quartz, but the remainder of the crystal refused to lose its milky hue. He tried several times, but nothing more than the face of the young man appeared.

"Set blast you, you cursed stone!"

The quartz did not seemed frightened by this threat; indeed, as if in response to the curse, even the face pictured therein faded, leaving the crystal once again blank.

Cursing further, Rey turned away from the obstinate crystal. Well, he thought, at least he had something: the danger to his domain seemed to be centered in that youthful face. Now he could prepare to deal with it.

"Wikkell!"

At the sound of the wizard's voice, something shuffled ponderously across the damp stone floor. Half again the size of a large man, the figure shambled into the eerie green light. It bore a single pink eye set in the middle of its sloping forehead, and upon its back, a hump, much like those worn by the desert-roaming beasts of the Southern Wastes bordering Punt and Stygia. Bald it was, but bearded, and dense muscle corded its arms and legs. The hunchback was naked save for a groin cloth; the knuckles of its hands nearly touched the stone under its splayed feet as it shuffled into sight.

"Master," the hunchbacked cyclops said. It had a voice like sail canvas being torn.

"Go to the Northern Chambers," Ray said, "and prepare a reception for anyone who ventures to cross the land above. I will have any who dare the forbidden paths brought before me."

"Master," Wikkell said by way of acknowledgment. He bowed slightly, causing his hands to scrape the floor, and turned to leave.

"Alive," Rey said to the retreating form. "I want them alive."

Chuntha the witch fondled the carved baculum wand and regarded her thrall. The Worm Gigantus lay before her, flattened on its bottom by its own weight. It looked as if someone had taken an ordinary red earthworm, increased its size by more than a thousandfold, and bleached it ghostly white. There were no features recognizable as a face—one end seemed much like the other—but a series of discolorations did indicate that the head of the giant worm faced Chuntha. Three times as long as a man's height and easily as thick as a wine barrel, the worm twitched as it listened to its mistress.

"Go, Deek," she said, "to the Northern Chambers. The danger to us will manifest itself there, and soon. We must control it to survive and triumph over That Bastard who opposes us. You are authorized to create an alliance with any who would aid us: the bats, the Whites, the Webspinners, any or all of them. Promise them what they ask, but do not allow the forces of That Bastard to obtain that which I seek. Do you understand?"

The worm could not speak, but by scraping its body in certain ways over the stone beneath it, the creature could manufacture a kind of counterfeit voice. "Y-y-yes-s."

When her servant had left, undulating its torpid body over the slimed floor, Chuntha stroked her cheek with the wand, thinking. She had not envisioned such a powerful dream in some time. The danger would come from a single man. She had seen that much, but not the face of the stranger. In the dim green light, she regarded the baculum. It had power, but perhaps not enough in this instance. Mayhap she needed to try the dreaming jewel. The ensorceled gem contained much magical force, and there was some risk involved in its use, but this was no time to be cautious. The signs portended great danger, and dangerous times required risky measures. Yes. She would fondle the dreaming jewel and see what insight it offered.

In the manse that perched upon the high rocks like a mountain goat, the Harskeel regarded itself in a floor-to-ceiling mirror, feeling for the first time in years a real sense of hope. That barbarian along the high road . . . could he be the one? Surely he was brave; he had faced six-to-one odds, even though his confederate had aided him. And the latest story, of how he had slain another in the village tavern with no more effort or worry than a man slaughtering sheep . . . surely that added to his bravery?

The Harskeel in the mirror nodded. Aye, it seemed to say, the blooded sword of this one might well be the final key we have been awaiting these last fifteen years. If this barbar—named Conan, according to its spies in the tavern—is the one, then we can be as we were before.

Yes. A pleasant thought.

Soon we shall have him, the Harskeel told itself. Already a score of our men prepare to ride. No matter how many must die, we *will* have that blade . . . and the blood of its bearer!

Certainly a pleasant thought.

* * *

The newly fallen snow enfolded the village like a white shroud, a pristine blanket that sparkled under an icy-blue sky. The storm had passed, leaving peace in its wake.

The sun had already completed a major portion of its morning's journey when Conan and Elashi emerged from the inn. They had breakfasted well; additionally, the innkeeper had supplied them with snowshoes so they might more easily traverse the knee-deep snows that had covered the road.

"We shall take the shorter route mentioned by the innkeeper," Conan said.

Elashi shook her head. "Did not you hear also the tale of the watchbeast that sometimes prowls that shorter path?"

"Aye. And Conan of Cimmeria is not prepared to march for an additional five days merely to avoid some escaped dog that 'sometimes prowls' a path." He patted his sword. "A blade that has slain a dire-wolf will certainly serve to dispatch some mangy cur should it trouble us."

"I did not hear the innkeeper say that the beast was a dog."

"What else? Perhaps the watchbeast is instead a goose. So much the better—then we shall dine in high style—should it honk threateningly at us." He laughed, amused by the image.

For once Elashi was quiet. Conan silently thanked Crom for not-so-small a favor.

So the pair marched away from the small village, high-stepping on their bentwood-and-gut snowshoes, hearing the dry powder beneath their feet squeak with each step. The day was bracing, if

cold, and Conan felt rested from his sleep and
belly-warm with his breakfast. Another two days
would see them clear of the Karpash mountains
and out of Corinthia, onto the Zamoran plateau. It
was but another half-moon's walk to Shadizar, so
he had been told. Less if he could steal a pair of
horses. Once there, Elashi would continue south-
ward and he could be about the business of enrich-
ing himself through serious thievery. He looked
forward to that with interest.

The twenty riders struggled to control their
mounts. The breath of men and animals made fog
in the freezing air as the horses shifted nervously
about.

Then the Harskeel itself entered the courtyard
astride its stallion. From its throat the deep voice
boomed out over the gathered riders. "I want the
man and his sword. A bag of gold coins to the one
who delivers them together. And a swift and painful death to any man who is the cause of their loss.
Is that perfectly clear?"

There came a murmur of assent from the riders.

"Good. We ride for the village. Now!"

The thunder of hooves shook the morning as the
Harskeel and its minions departed the manse's
courtyard.

Three hours out of the village, Conan and Elashi
paused to lunch upon strips of lamb jerky purchased at the inn. The meat was dry and chewy,
but fortunately the innkeeper had also supplied
the couple with a leather flask of mild wine, and
they used this to wash down the jerky. Later, when

they camped for the night, Conan could set snares for rabbits or ringtails, which they could roast over the evening's fire. With luck, they could be through the pass and over the mountain road's highest elevation by darkfall.

Wikkell, the hunchbacked cyclops, moved through narrow corridors of wet stone, splashing through puddles of limed water that sometimes bubbled with inner effervescence. There were a dozen ways to reach the Northern Chambers, this tunnel being one of the wider ones, albeit not the shortest. It would not do to be stuck in one of the narrow tubes whilst on Katamay Rey's business. The master held no interest in excuses, and he was not gentle with those who failed him. Wikkell's predecessor as first assistant had angered the wizard, and as a result, had spent his final moment of life turning into a puddle of putrid ooze upon Rey's chamber floor. Wikkell's first chore as new assistant had been to clean up the remains of his predecessor, an unpleasant task that ever cautioned him to take extreme care in dealing with the wizard who ruled half of the cave system.

Recalling that incident served to hurry Wikkell's splayed feet as he moved toward his goal. Should he fail in his assigned task, 'twould be better not to return to these parts at all; certainly it was an option he would keep in mind, but one he would rather not exercise. He increased his pace yet more.

Deek slithered along a twisting tunnel, moving quite fast for a being without appendages. The belly plates upon which he traveled had evolved to suit rock, and he slid forward more like a snake than a worm, winding from side to side, head slightly raised above the slimed floor of the cave.

As he crawled along, Deek formulated his plans for communication with the other sentient species that inhabited the Grotterium Negrotus. The Blood-bats lived to eat and procreate, and they always needed more room. He could offer them one of the giant caverns to the west of the cave complex as a breeding ground. Chuntha had kept them empty for reasons of her own, and the bats would do anything to occupy such a vast space.

The Webspinners, on the other coil, were permanently stationary, and grown thin from lack of proper food. Could Deek assure them of a steady food supply, they would be more than willing to aid the witch in any way they could.

And the Blind Whites? Well, they were quite another matter. Those obscene, apelike creatures were friendly with the cyclopes and unlikely to want anything Chuntha could supply. Like as not, they would pull rock daggers on any worm foolish enough to approach them, stabbing first and asking each other stupid questions as they ingested the remains. Best to avoid those vermin altogether.

Deek had not seen Chuntha so agitated since the worms had brought her that man traveler a few months past. She had practically danced then; unfortunately, the poor traveler had not lasted very long under the witch's ministrations, a single episode in her bed being enough to finish him. But the remains had been quite tasty, as Deek recalled. Perhaps the witch would allow them to have her leavings again once this new traveler had served his purpose. But first they had to catch him.

Deek increased his coiling, moving faster. It would not do to miss this person. Not at all. Deek had no desire to serve as fodder for the lime pits, a fate very likely to be the result of failing to please Chuntha.

Conan and Elashi rounded the trail's turning as the sun began to sink behind the tallest peak to the west. The trek had been monotonous thus far. They had seen no one save an occasional curious mountain goat peering down at them. Another hour or so and they could stop for the night, Conan figured.

Then, just ahead, from the hard shadow of a sharp-edged spire of rock, a monster stepped into their path.

Conan and Elashi stopped and stared at the beast. Big it was, as large as a draft horse, but save that it stood on four legs, altogether unlike any horse they had ever seen. The beast looked to have been assembled by some mad god intent on blending dog, cat, and rat. The head was mostly canine but with catlike jowls and teeth; the body wore striped fur, much like a domestic tabby's, but in contour it was more like a hunting hound. The tail was long and pink, naked of hair, and properly belonged on a giant rat. The feet were also ratlike, with four toes on each foot, and each toe was tipped with a black claw. The thing growled and emitted a short bark, sounding like a great grizzled bear.

Without taking her startled gaze from the monster, Elashi spoke. "Some mangy stray dog, you said? Or perhaps a fat goose upon which we could dine, eh? Once again you astound me with your predictive powers, Conan."

"Better you should use your blade than your mouth," Conan said, starting to reach for his own sword.

The thing gave another bearlike bark and sniffed the air. Conan froze, leaving his sword in place. The wind was at the watchbeast's back, as the outlander could tell from the stench reaching his nostrils. Perhaps it could not see particularly well, for it made no move toward them.

"It seems unsure of us," he said, dropping his voice to a whisper. "Perhaps if we remain still, it will lose interest."

"We might stand here until we starve," Elashi said, her voice also low.

"I am open to suggestion."

"Why do you always say that at such times as this?" Her voice grew somewhat louder.

"Why not yell, to better attract its attention?"

That shut her up. They stared at the composite beast.

For its part, the watchbeast did seem somewhat confused. It cocked its head from side to side, quizzically staring in Conan and Elashi's direction. Had it any sight at all, it seemed impossible that it would miss them, the distance being less than perhaps thirty spans; it sniffed the frosty air unmoving.

Conan's hand itched to pull his sword, but he remained still. Better to wait a few moments at least, to see what the thing would do. If it came at them, he would have plenty of time to draw his weapon, although fighting such a monster hardly seemed a pleasant pursuit.

The horseman touched the track in the snow, then turned to face the Harskeel and the other riders. "Very fresh, m'lord. The snow has kept the impression of the footwear's strings. They can be no more than a very few minutes ahead of us."

The Harskeel flashed its ambiguous smile. "Good. Forward!"

"Have you gods we can call upon?" Elashi whispered.

"None but Crom," Conan said. "And Crom rarely listens to prayers. He gives a man strength and cunning in certain measure at birth, then allows him to make his own way in the world."

"A harsh god," Elashi said.

"Aye. He rules over a harsh land, he could be little else."

"My own gods tend to be good for finding water or helping with the hunt," she said. "I don't think we have any god for dealing with the likes of that." She gestured at the beast with a glance. The thing had by this time sat upon its haunches, still staring in the direction of the two unmoving people.

"I cannot understand why it does not merely approach closer to see what we are," Conan said.

"Let us not give it any ideas in that direction, Conan."

"We cannot stay here forever," he said. "Perhaps we can utilize the same trick we played upon the Harskeel. I shall run aslant to it and when it chases me, you can attack it from the rear."

"A good idea," she said quickly.

Conan could not suppress a small chuckle. She did not hurry to volunteer to draw this beast's attention, he noted.

"Of course, once I move, it might notice us both," Conan said. "And mayhap choose to take the stationary meal instead."

Elashi considered this for all of three seconds. "On second thought, I think perhaps your plan lacks merit. Let us both draw our blades and run directly at it."

"Aye, better than to die a frozen statue. Ready?"

"As I shall ever be."

"Your sword, then."

As Conan and Elashi unsheathed their weapons, the watching monster came to its feet. Its striped fur bristled and it uttered several more barks, followed by a rumbling growl. The two were starting to run, when they heard another sound.

"There they are!"

Conan glanced over his shoulder to see a horde of horsemen bearing down upon them.

"Crom! What is this?"

Elashi did not question her fortunes, however. She merely took off at a right angle to the trail, diving behind a clump of scraggly brush. Conan understood. He duplicated the desert woman's dive and crouched down behind the weedy cover in time to see the watchbeast go sprinting past, heading straight for the approaching horsemen.

The bearlike cries and growls joined the yells of startled men and the whinny of terrified horses.

The watchbeast leaped, knocked three riders from their mounts and began to claw and chew the downed men, rending them as easily as a wolf does a hare. The other men began throwing pikes, some of which struck the monster, injuring and enraging it.

Conan saw at the rear of the pack of men and animals none other than the Harskeel itself, gesturing and screaming at its men.

"I think it best that we depart," Conan said, pointing at the fracas.

"For once I agree."

Quickly, the two of them hurried away from the fight.

Ten minutes away from the battle behind them, Conan and Elashi slowed their pace somewhat. "I think the Harskeel will have its hands full binding wounds," he said. "Besides, they will not be able to follow us in the dark. Nightfall is only moment away. We are safe for now."

Elashi nodded. "The Harskeel must indeed consider you a prime candidate for its magic."

"Aye, but . . . who knows? Mayhap it considers *you* a candidate as well. You also bear a sword."

That thought made her stop and think for a moment.

"We shall continue walking through the night," Conan said. "By morning we should be clear of the mountain and able to take any direction we choose on the plateau. They won't be able to follow us if we take pains to cover our trail."

"Then you feel we are in no danger?"

"I have no doubt of it," Conan said, smiling.

Just then the ground opened beneath them, swallowing them like the maw of some giant creature.

Four

The length of their fall was nearly five spans; fortunately, the bottom of the descent was watery. Conan splashed into an icy pool and sank, quickly touching the bottom. He pushed away and broke the surface, realizing that he could easily stand as the depth was equal only to his chest. Elashi's head appeared briefly above the surface as she came up yelling; then she began to sink again. Apparently her rearing in the desert had not included instruction in the art of swimming. Conan grabbed one of Elashi's wildly waving hands and pulled her to him. She immediately clamped her legs around his waist and wound her arms tightly around his neck, sputtering incoherently.

The Cimmerian took stock. The pool was no more than a small pond in size, occupying a portion of what was obviously a tunnel in a cavern. The walls of this rock tube appeared to be as smooth as a child's face, and curved upward in tight arcs that, combined with the lack of projections, offered no means by which to climb. Cimmerians learned to climb almost as soon as they learned to walk, and if one of them could see no way of ascending something, likely it could not be done. Were the ceiling closer, he could perhaps toss Elashi up to the hole there, and she might then dangle knotted clothing or a vine down to Conan for him to climb up. Yes, and were lizards winged, why, then they would be birds.

The thickening night above offered less light with every moment. Best they leave this freezing water as soon as possible, Conan thought, and find another exit before darkness enshrouded them totally. He began to wade from the pool to the nearest shore, Elashi's weight being small burden on his efforts.

"Crom!"

Elashi leaned back from her tight embrace to look at Conan's face. "What it is?"

Conan did not answer but nodded toward the shadows of the cave. Elashi turned slightly to see what had drawn the oath from the Cimmerian.

Moving into the fast-dwindling light from out of the hidden depths of the cave came a double handful of . . . things. White they were, squat creatures more kin to ape than human. They wore no clothing save their own shaggy fur, and while each face showed a nose and mouth, where their eyes would be were only blank flesh and bone. They bore very large ears, however.

"Mitra!" Elashi said.

The water now stood below Conan's knees. He increased his pace, to reach the shore before the eyeless white creatures would arrive. Elashi relaxed her hold upon Conan and reached for her sword. Conan drew his own weapon as the two of them attained the drier, but still damp stone floor.

"Perhaps they are friendly," Elashi said. She did not sound particularly convinced.

"Perhaps," Conan said. "But let us keep our blades ready in case they are not."

She did not argue with that.

The blind white creatures moved closer.

The Harskeel was enraged: six of its men dead, two more dying, and another three wounded badly enough to require that they quit the chase. Only nine remained uninjured after slaying the hellish beast that had attacked them. The barbarian and the woman had escaped; night staked its claim to the day even as the Harskeel had its troops lay a rough camp. Damnation! The quarry had been within their grasp! Now they would have to wait until first light to proceed—who knew if the slain monster had a mate or kin in the hills?—and the Harskeel would bet gold against goat dung that Conan and the female with him would not dally, awaiting their pursuers. By the Nameless and all of its furry minions! Knowing there was nothing to be done for it decreased the Harskeel's rage not one whit.

* * *

Wikkell was weakening the cave roof for yet another pitfall trap when one of the Blind Whites ran into the chamber and skittered to a stop against the heavy ladder upon which the cyclops stood precariously balanced.

"Idiot!" Wikkell yelled as the ladder swayed.

The Blind White chittered something in its own language, a tongue that Wikkell had been required to learn in order to perform his duties for Katamay Rey.

"What? What are you babbling about?"

The creature repeated its hastily blurted speech, and this time Wikkell was able to make sense of it. The man, the one they sought, had fallen into the trap below the pass's summit!

Wikkell hastened to scramble down the ladder. Success, and so soon! The wizard would be pleased. "Do you have him?"

The Blind White assured Wikkell that this was so. Ten of his brothers surrounded the trapped man and would doubtless already be bearing him to one of the lock chambers in the Whites' main cave.

"Good, good!" With that, Wikkell shuffled off after the Blind White to fetch his quarry.

Deek heard the tale from a leathery-brown Bloodbat, who swooped down to perch on a stalagmite nearby. Deek did not particularly trust the bats, since they were always willing to switch allegiance to whomever offered the most reward; still, at the moment the monkey-sized bats seemed prone to work for Chuntha . . . after the generous offer of breeding space.

Deek dragged that portion of himself that passed for a vocal apparatus over the rock. "A-are y-y-you s-sure?"

Certain, the bat affirmed. A pair of blood-filled humans had fallen into One Eye's traps: a large and likely delicious meaty one, and a smaller tidbit.

Deek agitated his scraper back and forth rapidly. "Wh-what h-h-happened to th-the m-m-men?"

As to that, the bat did not know for certain. The report from the overflier was that the two succulent morsels had been surrounded by a large group of the Blind Whites, intent on their capture.

"D-damn!"

Deek twisted his bulk and began undulating along the floor. If One Eye had the men, Deek was a prime candidate for the lime pit. Not a pleasant fate. He had to do something, and quickly! The Webspinner Plants were thick in this portion of the cave system. Perhaps he could enlist their aid. He must do something, in order to continue his existence. Without the one the witch sought, Deek's life was worth less than the guano beneath that wretched and stupid bat!

The first of the eyeless white things sprang, less carefully than it should have. They were definitely not friendly, Conan decided as he sidestepped and swung his sword in a flat horizonal arc. The end of the blade tore through the creature's side, cutting it very nearly in twain. It continued its leap past Conan and fell into the pool behind the man. The blood was red enough, even in the dying light; ruby stained the cold ripples.

The rest of the attackers moved more cautiously.

When Conan edged forward, they gave ground, spreading out to try and surround the Cimmerian and Elashi.

Then Conan noticed an odd thing. As the light from above faded, he saw an eerie greenish glow coming from the walls and ceiling of the chamber; it was a ghostly pale luminescence, but sufficient for the Cimmerian's sharp eyes to see clearly.

The surrounding creatures seemed in no hurry to move, and Conan decided that 'twould be better if he and Elashi departed. He said so.

"And how are we to accomplish that? Fly over them?"

"Nay," Conan said, taking a firmer grip on his sword's haft. "Not over, but through. There are only three of them blocking the way. You take the one on the right and I shall clear the other two from the path. On my signal."

Elashi sighed, licked her lips, and nodded.

"Now!"

With that, the two of them leaped at the three startled creatures. Elashi's target simply turned and ran, while Conan's both emitted startled growls and crashed into each other in their efforts to get out of his way. There came the sound of bone meeting bone as their skulls connected. They fell, and Conan sprang over them and found himself running next to Elashi.

"That was not so difficult," Elashi said.

Conan managed a grunt but saved the rest of his breath for running.

Into the depths of the glowing tunnel they fled, pursued by the rest of the chittering creatures.

*   *   *

Wikkell stood over the floating corpse of the Blind White, staring at it. He blinked his single pink eye, then turned to the two Blind Whites who sat on the cold floor rubbing at lumps on their heads.

"What happened to the men?" Wikkell finally asked.

The two Whites babbled. The things were monsters, they said. They chopped down one of the brothers with giant claws—you could hear the whistle as they swung their weapons!—and sought to rend us likewise! We stood in their path and they hurled us aside like you would brush a spider away! We fought valiantly but were overcome by the power of the monsters . . .

"Enough," Wikkell said. "You let them escape."

But our brothers pursue, the two said.

"You had better pray they catch them," Wikkell said. "If those humans escape, it will be my life. Before I go, I will take you and as many of your brothers as I can with me!"

Upon them the curses of ten thousand demons! Wikkell moved down the tunnel into which the men had fled. He already knew that the witch had sent one of her fat worms wiggling this way to fetch his quarry. If she got it, he would spend the rest of his life waiting for the wizard's curse that would convert him to melting ooze. Not that the wait would be all that long. He had to capture the man Rey desired, no two ways about it.

Deek emerged into the wide section of the tunnel and observed with his hidden eyes the form of

a dead Blind White bobbing in the pool beneath
the opening to the sky.

The bat who had spoken to him earlier spiraled
down and landed upon the corpse, which promptly
sank. The bat squawked and lifted, to alight once
again on the edge of the pond.

"D-d-don't b-b-bother," Deek said. "Th-that
o-one's b-blood is m-m-mostly g-gone."

Well, something was better than nothing, the
bat said. If the mighty Deek would help fetch the
tidbit in the water, why, then the bat would tell
him something interesting.

The mighty Deek's anger flared, and for a moment he considered dropping a coil onto the bat
and reducing it to a mashed blood spot upon the
floor. The image of the lime pit intruded, and he
thought better of it. Raising his tail and snapping
it down sharply, Deek slapped the water behind
the dead Blind White. The splash hurled the body
and half of the pond's water into the air. When the
dead creature landed, the Bloodbat was on it in an
instant, stabbing the pointed tube through which
it fed into the cooling corpse.

"Y-y-you h-had s-s-something t-to t-tell m-me?"
Deek scraped from the rock as he loomed over the
bat.

The creature jerked its feeding tube from the
body; blood dripped from the angled tip. Oh, yes,
it said. Those two humans Deek wanted? Well,
they had escaped from the Blind Whites and One
Eye. They went that way.

Deek could not believe his good fortune. Escaped?
That meant there was still a chance that he could
capture them! Filled with sudden hope, Deek slid

away at full crawl. Mayhap he could escape the lime pit after all!

In his chamber, Katamay Rey waited for word of the man's capture. He had thought to have Wikkell dispatch the man immediately, but on re-thinking it, decided that perhaps it would be wiser to question the captive. Likely as not, a single person could not cause all the grief the wizard had foreseen in his crystal. More likely the man repre-sented another magician, or perhaps some army; better to keep him alive long enough to ascertain the truth. Then he could kill him. And there were some spells that called for human blood and body parts, of course; so he would not be wasted. The wizard smiled at his cleverness. Soon this little incident would be finished and he could get back to the business of grinding That Bitch into well-deserved oblivion.

Chuntha touched the dreaming jewel, a fire-filled ruby, to various parts of her body, groaning with the pleasure it gave. The gem did not tell her when Deek would return with the captives, but it did say that there would be more than one involved in this matter. Chuntha beheld blurry images of an-other; perhaps two or three more. That boded ill. One was bad enough. She must take care to be certain that the wizard did not come by this knowledge.

She smiled into the putrid phosphor enveloping her. The one central to this business was a man of great physical power, the jewel told her. Young and strong and vibrant, alive with raw male energy, he would be a welcome treat after the recent months of drought. To lie with one such as the jewel bespoke would add greatly to her power. The Sensha would wrap them in its embrace, and the man's being would flow into hers, physically and spiritually. It promised to be the most exciting encounter in quite some time.

Chuntha could hardly wait!

Meanwhile, along corridors lined with rocky teeth above and below, Conan and Elashi sprinted, trying to lose their pursuers. As they ran, they descended deeper into the earth; around them, the air grew colder.

High above, night draped its ebon cloak over the land, but it mattered not the least in the fungus-lined depths of the cave that seemed to have no end.

Five

The morning sun cast its light over the mountain trail, the beams bright but offering little heat in the clear wintry air. The Harskeel watched from horseback as one of its men leaned over the hole in the ground. Two other men held the first's feet as he dangled into the pit. After a moment the two supporters pulled the man up. He stood and faced the Harskeel.

"There be a cave under the trail, m'lord. Big 'un. The tracks end at the edge, so it looks like the two of 'em fell in. Pretty long drop down there. There be water at the bottom."

The Harskeel shifted on its saddle, eliciting a creak from the stiff leather. "No sign of them?"

"Nay, m'lord."

"Could they have survived the drop? Is the water deep enough to ensure that?"

The man shook his head. "Can't say, m'lord."

The Harskeel nodded at the two men behind the speaker, gesturing with a small jerk of its head, pointing into the pit with its nose. They understood. Before the speaker could gather his wits, the other two stepped forward and shoved him. He stumbled and pitched over the edge of the pit, screaming. Came a splash; then, after a moment, a curse.

"Hmm," the Harskeel said. "It seems as if they could have survived such a fall. Very well. They are likely alive then. We shall construct ladders and torches. They are down there, and so shall we go likewise."

The men looked nervous at this suggestion, but the Harskeel did not care. It felt certain. This Conan was the one to supply the ingredient to lift the spell. Oh, to be two again!

"Be quick about it," the Harskeel ordered.

An hour later a makeshift ladder was lowered into the cave. Leaving a single man to watch the horses, the Harskeel and its remaining troops descended into the pit.

The blind followers were persistent but not nearly as fleet of foot as Conan and Elashi. While the Cimmerian and the desert woman had not lost their pursuers, they had gained a considerable lead as they ran through the twists and turns of the cavern's corridors. Thus far they had been fortunate not to have fled down a dead end or into a tube that narrowed so much as to forbid passage.

With the last turning, however, their luck seemed to expire. At the end of the corridor were two passages; the one on the right narrowed almost immediately, so that they would have to crawl down it. The passage to the left was larger, but a thundering waterfall obscured one wall of that tunnel, and the water gathered in what appeared to be deep pools beneath the cascade, blocking the path. Recalling Elashi's swimming abilities, it did not look to be a promising route.

"We had better go back to the last turning," Elashi said, voicing Conan's thought.

"Too late," he said. "Even now the floor vibrates with their footsteps." He unsheathed his sword. "It appears we must take our stand here."

Elashi nodded and drew her sword. She and Conan stood side by side, waiting for the white beasts.

"This way," came a man's voice over the sound of the cataract.

Conan spun around. He saw no one.

"Here," came the voice again.

Squinting into the left-hand corridor, Conan was startled to see a man's hand emerge from the near side of the waterfall. The hand beckoned. "Hurry!" the voice said.

Conan and Elashi glanced at each other. They had little to lose. Even so, the big Cimmerian approached the roaring water cautiously, finding that the deep pool in the center of the corridor was bounded by a shallow ledge. Once he attained the spot where he had seen the hand, Conan leaped through, his blade held ready to strike.

Behind the waterfall, which was wide but shallower than it had appeared, a short, thick-set man stood, illuminated by the green glow of the ubiquitous wall fungus. Old he was, perhaps fifty, with a gray beard and long, matted gray hair under a limp hat. His clothes were soggy cloth breeches and shirt, and crude sandals, and he held a long dagger at the ready. Behind the man lay a high corridor, winding away for a long distance.

Elashi splashed through behind Conan, water spraying from her form. As soon as she looked up, the older man gestured with his head down the corridor. Conan needed no prompting to understand. They followed the stranger away from the waterfall.

Around two turns of the corridor, the man stopped. "Them Blind Whites can't hear us through the noise of the waterfall, and they can't smell nothin' past the water, neither. They won't come this way."

"We thank you for your aid," Conan said.

"Tull, I'm called," the old man said.

"Well met, and timely, Tull. I'm Conan, of Cimmeria, and this is Elashi, of Khauran." The Cimmerian paused, then asked, "What is this place, friend?"

"That'll take some time for the tellin'."

Conan looked around. "It seems that we have little else."

"I have a hiding place not far from here," Tull said. "Suppose we go there and I'll explain what I know."

Conan and Elashi nodded. Tull moved off, and they followed.

Wikkell ducked to avoid a crusty stalagtite dangling from the low ceiling. His Blind White guide stopped, cocked his head to one side, then turned to the cyclops. The guide chattered. His fellows were returning, it seemed. They approached from down the corridor and would be upon them momentarily.

Wikkell smiled at that, revealing thick, wide-set teeth. This venture was proving to be easier than he had anticipated. In a moment the Blind Whites would appear—there they were now—and they would be bearing with them—

No one!

Where were the men?

The leader of the Whites shuffled his feet on the floor. There had been two of them, he said, one a female, judging from her odor. But they had escaped.

"Escaped!" Wikkell roared the word as if it were a virulent curse.

That was so. Vanished into solid rock.

"Men do not vanish into solid rock," the cyclops said.

Either that or they walked on water, the leader of the group said. Perhaps they were wizards.

"Show me. I will see this with my own eye."

A waste of time, the leader said.

"It is my time to waste." And, he thought to himself, if the quarry has truly escaped, there will be considerably less time remaining to me than heretofore.

The cyclops followed the Blind Whites down the corridor.

The bat alighted upon a rocky fold just ahead of Deek and used its teeth to scratch at something on its left wing strut.

"W-w-what i-is t-t-the n-n-news-s-s?

Bad, the bat told the worm. The two men—one a female, so he had learned by listening to that barbaric speech of the Whites—had escaped, vanished, disappeared.

Deek considered that. It was bad that he did not have the man and woman in his possession; on the other coil, it was good that One Eye did not have them either. Perhaps this affair might be salvaged yet.

"I-i-is t-t-there a-a-another w-way t-to w-w-where t-the m-m-men v-v-vanished-d-d?" This was a long speech for Deek to scratch out on the rock.

The bat indicated that this was so.

"S-sh-show m-m-me."

In his chamber, Katamay Rey grew impatient, waiting for news of the man's capture. He rummaged through his collection of crystals, searching for the small blue stone that he used for communication. He would call his cyclops and ask about the delay.

Where was that cursed stone?

In her chamber, Chuntha fumed, awaiting the report from her minion Deek. What could be keeping him? She would give him another hour; then she would try a dreamcast to contact the great white worm. The anticipation of receiving the captive was high in her, and she was not one to suffer delay easily.

Tull's hiding place proved to be a fungoid grotto reached by climbing up a rough wall in a large cave. The narrow entrance to the grotto was covered by a flap of hide that had been covered with crushed stone so that it blended into the wall, rendering it almost invisible from the floor of the cave below.

Inside, the walls were caked thick with the glowing fungus; here the light was concentrated and almost bright. The room contained a small table constructed of various lengths of bone bound with gut strings, upon it rested a cup made from an animal's skull. There was also a pile of furs in one corner, likely used for sleeping. Conan noted that these furs seemed very similar in shape and color to the Blind Whites, as Tull had called them. Also, there were smaller skins, birdlike but rat-colored, in the collection.

"This place is called the Grotterium Negrotus," Tull said. "The Black Caves. I have been here for nearly five years, best as I can figure."

"How did you come to be so?" Elashi asked.

"I fell through a hole in the ground above."

"Sounds familiar," she said.

"Who were those creatures that attacked us?" Conan asked.

"Them's the Blind Whites. Mostly they side with Rey."

"Rey?"

"Aye. There's two rulers down here. One's Katamay Rey, he's a wizard what uses crystals and such for his magic. The other's Chuntha the witch. Her magic, well, it's more involved with, uh—" he glanced at Elashi—"uh, it's more of a *personal* nature."

"Personal nature?" Elashi asked.

Tull made a sign with his hands, the meaning of which was unmistakable. Conan grinned, and Elashi glared at him.

"Anyways, the two of 'em have been at each other for as long as I been here. According to what I heard, they been fightin' each other for control of the caves for hundreds of years. Got all the natives workin' for 'em. Blind Whites, which you met, Webspinner Plants, Bloodbats, Worms Gigantus, and the hunchbacked cyclopes. They switch sides sometimes."

"Sounds like a wonderful place," Elashi said, her voice full of irony. "Why do you stay here?"

"Can't get out. The worms 'n' the cyclopes, they close up the trap holes after a little while. In five years I ain't found a way out."

Conan stared at Tull. To be trapped here for the rest of one's life? That was an unpleasant thought.

"I get by," Tull continued. "Nobody's found this place, and the taste of the Whites and bats ain't so bad once you get used to it."

"Are there any other people here?"

Tull shook his head. "Now and again somebody drops in through one of the traps. If Rey gets 'em, he kills 'em quick and that's it for 'em. If Chuntha gets 'em, the goin' is more pleasant, judging from what I heard and seen once, but almost as fast.

Druther be caught by her 'n' him, but I avoid 'em both."

Conan digested this morsel of information. "I have no intention of spending my days in this pit," he said. "We shall have to find a way out."

"I been lookin' for five years and ain't found it yet."

"Nonetheless, there must be a way."

"You'll want to be careful," Tull said. "If the Whites know, then Rey knows you're down here and likely anything Rey knows, Chuntha will know, too. They'll be lookin' for you."

Conan touched the handle of his sword. "Perhaps they might be sorry if they find me," he said.

Tull glanced at Conan's sword, then at the big Cimmerian's muscular frame. "Aye, perhaps. But likely you'll be sorrier. One cyclops would make two of you, and there's hundreds of 'em. And the big worms can sometimes squeeze the air out of a cyclops, one against one."

Conan and Elashi looked at each other.

"Better we should find a way out," Elashi said.

Conan said nothing, but agreed silently. Witches, wizards, and hellish cavern beasts held no attraction for him whatsoever. The sooner they left this place, the better Conan would like it.

Six

The size of the cave system impressed the Harskeel while at the same time frightening its men. Their torches cast a fitful yellow glow that blended with the fungal green light emitted from the dank walls. Finding Conan and the woman might prove to be a more difficult task than first the Harskeel had imagined. Well, it made no difference. Conan was the one; the Harskeel grew more convinced of it every moment. Once it had the barbarian's sword, the spell reversing this accursed joining could be intoned. The words had long since been committed to the Harskeel's memory, burned in deeply as if placed there by a red-hot iron brand.

Ahead, the tracker uttered a short curse.

"What is it?" the Harskeel asked.

"Lost the sign agin, m'lord. Looks like somethin' passed behind 'em and wiped it away. See?"

The tracker held his torch close to the floor. The encrusted salts and slime had been smoothed over, as if something wide and heavy had been dragged over the surface in a side-to-side manner. There was a kind of pattern to the smoothing, a widened "S" shape.

"Ever see a track like this before?" the Harskeel asked.

The tracker shook his head. "Can't say's I have, m'lord. Not exactly. Once, in the desert, I seen a pattern kinda like it. Serpent track. But there ain't no snakes this size." He gestured at the floor.

You hope, the Harskeel thought. And I hope so too. 'Twould be difficult to utilize Conan and his blade did they have to be extracted from the belly of a monster serpent.

"We shall continue on down this tunnel," the Harskeel said.

The Whites had moved ahead of Wikkell toward the waterfall cavern and so the cyclops was alone when the call came from his master. All of a moment the air to one side of the cave seemed to swirl with purple light; a low humming began and increased in volume to that of a giant winged insect. Wikkell stopped, realizing almost immediately the cause of the phenomenon.

From the purple haze came Rey's voice. "HAVE YOU THE MAN I SEEK?"

Wikkell swallowed dryly and chose his words carefully. "Even now I am on my way to collect him, Master. The Blind Whites have trapped him in a corridor some distance away."

"HOW LONG UNTIL YOU RETURN WITH HIM?"

"Ah, that is difficult to predict, Master. The corridor is some distance away, as I said. And your chambers are considerably farther, as the man is in the opposite direction from them."

"MAKE HASTE, WIKKELL. I HATE TO BE KEPT WAITING."

"I shall return as soon as possible, Master."

The purple blot upon the air swirled and faded, leaving the cyclops alone in the dim green light. He tried to swallow again but found his mouth too dry to accomplish that simple task. He had purchased more time with his lie ... well, perhaps not a lie, only an exaggeration. But best he hurry and accomplish that which he had told Rey was imminent. Otherwise....

The image of himself as a steaming puddle of ooze upon the floor thrust itself into the cyclops' thoughts. He increased his speed.

Though he was wide awake, Deek had a dream. In it he lay at the feet of Chuntha, who loomed over him as if she were ten times her normal size. "Where are the people I sent you to fetch?" she demanded.

Deek could feel himself exude the oily flux that passed for sweat among his kind. "I—I h-have n-not yet a-arrived at t-t-their l-location, M-m-mistress. I-it is ... ah ... s-s-some d-distance a-away."

Chuntha increased in size, towering over Deek. She bent and picked up the worm as if he were no more than a hatching fresh from the egg. She held him in her hands as she sometimes did that wand-bone of hers. With the slightest pressure, she could squeeze him into mush. "Hurry, Deek. I grow impatient. You do not want that."

Without a sounding rock to scrape upon, Deek could not speak, but no, he definitely did not want Chuntha impatient with him. No.

Deek awoke to find himself crawling along as before, the bat, his guide, still flitting back and forth above him. Had he the ability, he would have sighed. In lieu of that, he merely increased his speed.

Conan had listened to Tull's story with interest, but he was not ready to accept the older man's conclusion. And were he to find the way out, best he begin looking immediately. He said as much.

Once again to his surprise, Elashi failed to contradict him. "Aye," she said. "The sooner we are shut of this place, the better."

Tull shook his head. "I think you're daft, lad, but I'll not see you wandering about in the caves without my assistance. May be that you can do what I could not. You shall have my knife's help."

Conan grinned. This was more like it. Far better to be up and doing something than to sit passively awaiting Fate's bidding. "Good," he said. "Then let us be about it."

With that, the three departed Tull's grotto.

Wikkell stood staring at the waterfall. "Are you certain they went this way?"

The Blind Whites affirmed that this was so.

The cyclops brooded for a moment. Well, if they went this way, he could also go thus. He began to wade into the icy water. It deepened quickly, rising as he stepped into it. Three paces and the water level was nearly at his chin. Too deep for the humans to have waded through it. Perhaps near the edge it was shallower . . . ?

Indeed. As Wikkell sidestepped, the pool's floor angled upward. In a moment the water was only knee-depth. It was tricky going, with that rushing cascade right next to him. He moved his splayed feet over the slippery bottom with care. The fugitives must have edged along like this until they were past the waterfall.

Wikkell slipped on a protruding bottom stone. He would have fallen into the depths of the pool, but he waved his arms wildly and instead overbalanced toward the flowing waterfall. He fell into it—

And through it.

Ho-ho! he thought as he drew himself to his feet and stood erect. The water hid another chamber and tunnel! He turned and stuck his head through the waterfall, now seen to be little more than a thin but wide cascading sheet.

"This way, blind fools," he said. "They went this way."

From a shallow crevasse in the stone floor, Deek watched as One Eye first disappeared into the waterfall, then pushed his head through it and called to the Blind Whites.

When the creatures had all moved through the

sheet of rushing water, the bat flitted down and alighted next to Deek.

"D-d-did y-y-ou k-know of t-this?"

The bat affirmed that it did. The other end of the tunnel entered into one of the Bloodbats' breeding chambers, in point of fact.

"I-is t-there a-a-another w-way to the c-c-chamber?"

Certainly, the bat said. You do not think that we fly through that water whenever we wish to leave, do you?

"T-t-take m-me t-t-there."

As you wish, the bat said, seeming bored by it all.

Deek felt a small surge of happiness as he slithered off after the supercilious bat. The prey would not be coming back this way, not with One Eye and the Whites blocking egress. If he could get to the other end in time, he could be there to capture them. With the help of a breeding cave full of bats, it should be easy enough.

"What lies at the ends of this tunnel?" Conan asked.

Tull pointed. "That way is the bat cave, where they breed. The other way you already know about; it's the waterfall."

"Is it possible to slip past the bats?" Elashi asked.

"Aye, lady, if one is careful and quiet. Mostly they sleep, when they ain't breeding."

"Then let us go that way," Conan said. As young as he was, his voice carried a tone of command. It was all well and good to joke with Elashi when they were ambling along a mountain trail, but when real danger threatened, Conan's instincts would not be thwarted by words. He would play her games only as long as it suited him.

Conan took the lead, with Elashi and Tull following.

The journey to the breeding cavern took less than an hour. As they neared their destination, Tull halted them and began to whisper.

"The bats do not see well," Tull said. "But they sense movement. Slow motions hardly register. If you think one sees you, hold still, and like as not it'll drift back to sleep without bothering you."

Conan nodded, noting that Elashi did the same.

"One thing, though," Tull said. "They can smell blood a long way off. If you get a scrape or cut, they'll be on you like flies on offal—no offense, lady—and there'll be hell to pay. Four or five of 'em can drain a White dry in a minute, and there's likely a hundred of 'em hanging from the ceiling in this cave. Take care you don't brush against a sharp rock."

Conan drew his sword.

"That won't do you no good," Tull said. "Not if you face a hundred of 'em."

"Perhaps not," Conan said. "But if they come to drink my blood, they will pay dearly with their own."

Tull chose not to speak to this, and with Conan still in the lead, they moved off.

Wikkell asked, "Do you know where this tunnel leads?" and realized the futility of the question before the chattering Whites could frame a reply.

Of course they did not know; until he had shown them, they had not realized the passageway even existed. Well, he would find out soon enough.

"H-h-how l-long?"

Soon, the bat said. Can you not smell the breeding chamber's lovely essence?

Deek did notice a foul, musty odor wafting down the hallway, but fortunately, had not complained of it.

"That smooth track turns and goes this way, m'lord."

The Harskeel nodded. It had a feeling that whatever had made that track would lead them to Conan. "Stay with it," the Harskeel ordered.

The bats were larger than Conan had anticipated. They hung upside down from protrusions on the roof and walls of the chamber, enwrapped in membranous wings so that they looked like giant flat-faced, tailless rats more than anything else. Here and there a pair were joined together, but for the most part, the hanging bats were still and quiet.

Slowly, carefully, the trio moved across the cave. There were rocks strewn all over, which made for dangerous footing, and spires of rock jutted up from the floor like talons waiting to snag an unwary victim.

More than a dozen openings led away from the cave, some of them at floor level, others higher up along the glowing green walls. There were three such exits directly across from where the trio had entered, and it was for the center opening that Conan, Tull, and Elashi made their way. Tull had indicated that this was the longest and largest of the local hallways, with abundant hiding places should someone or some*thing* come along.

They were halfway across the large cavern, the bats overhead sleeping peacefully, when trouble arrived. And as trouble was wont to do, it arrived in droves.

Behind them, a gravelly voice said, "There! Get them!"

Conan spun about, sword at the ready. From the tunnel they had recently vacated, eight or ten of the Blind Whites poured forth, chattering. Behind them lumbered a creature unlike anything the Cimmerian had ever seen. Tall it was, half again Conan's own height, with a hunched back and a single pink eye. It shambled forward, as fast as the Whites for all its size, gnarled and muscular arms outstretched, fingers splayed wide as if to gather in Conan and his friends.

The leading Blind White chose that moment to trip upon a loose rock. He fell, and misfortune guided him so that he was impaled upon one of the stalagmite talons, the point of which emerged from the hapless creature's back.

If the sounds of the chattering Whites had not been enough to awaken the bats, the gout of blood from the clumsy one certainly was. Overhead, the bats came to life.

There was more. Behind Conan, Tull swore. Conan spared him a glance and in the background saw a single bat emerge from another tunnel, followed by—Crom!—a ghostly pale worm as big around as a man! The beast slithered across the rocky floor toward the three people, bent on its own hellish purpose.

As the bats began to swoop down, screeching in high-pitched voices, the Blind Whites snatched up rocks from the floor and hurled them at the flying creatures. Though they must have been aiming at the sounds, their throws were none the less accurate than if they had eyes. Bats were struck by the stones and knocked from the air.

"The men, get the men!" the cyclops yelled, its voice a roar. The Whites, however, were too busy to pay the one-eyed creature much heed.

A bat flew at Conan, and the Cimmerian slashed with his blade, hacking one wing off. The bat spiraled away, screeching.

"There he is!" came another voice.

Conan looked for the source of this new threat. From the tunnel behind the great white worm came seven or eight men, armed with pikes and carrying torches. Conan recognized them a heartbeat before their leader appeared. The Harskeel!

The bats also noted this new intrusion into their nesting area, and it seemed no more pleasing than the others. Dozens of them swooped down upon the pikemen and the Harskeel. The men jabbed and cut at the flying creatures with their short pikes, but to little effect.

Bats screeched, Whites chittered, the Harskeel and his men screamed, the cyclops roared, and the giant worm scraped across the rock. Pandemonium ruled the cave.

"Best we leave!" Tull shouted as Conan chopped another diving bat from the air.

Conan swung his sword again, barely missing yet another bat. Aye, now there was an idea whose time had come.

Seven

Departing from the bat-infested cavern was not as easy to do as to say. As Conan slew still another darting bat, something leaped upon his back. He twisted, hurling one of the Blind Whites to the floor. Elashi finished the creature with a thrust of her blade. Blood gouted.

"This way!" Tull yelled.

Moving on a surface made slippery by gore, Conan and Elashi sought to follow the older man.

One of the pikemen managed to slog his way toward them, brandishing his weapon. "Halt!" he called. Then "Urk!" as both a bat and a Blind White fastened themselves to him.

Behind Conan, the giant cyclops roared and used

his massive fists like hammers, battering aside men, bats, and Whites foolish enough to get in his way.

To Conan's left, the sluglike worm crawled closer, swatting at the occasional White with the tip of what the Cimmerian assumed to be its tail. That segment of the worm whipped through the air with more speed than the young Cimmerian would have thought possible, smashing the apelike creatures, spinning them away like children's dolls.

Conan cut another bat from the air, slinging its hot blood into Elashi's face. "Watch what you are doing!" she yelled.

Tull said, "Here!"

Conan and the desert woman hurried through the sudden clearing of antagonists to the tunnel in which Tull stood, urging them to him. In another moment they had made their exit.

Running down the tunnel, Conan asked, "Where are we going?"

"Does it matter?" Elashi said. "Away from that place!"

"This tunnel has a number of twists and branches," Tull called out, a wheeze in his voice. "We can lose any pursuit here."

"Perhaps they will not pursue us at all."

"I think that might be wishful thinking, lass. It strikes me that all of 'em are after you and the big 'un here."

"Wonderful," Elashi muttered. "Just wonderful."

The Harskeel was willing to allow all of its men to die could it but attain its prey, but there was no point in permitting them to be slaughtered without achieving that goal. The tunnel into which Conan and the girl—and that old man, who was he?—had fled was all the way across a cavern full of strange creatures bent upon destruction. Best to retreat and gather his energies for a later pursuit, the Harskeel told itself.

"To me!" it called.

Only four pikemen were able to respond, and the Harskeel, bloody sword in hand, led them to the nearest exit. On the way, they gathered up one of the wounded bats. Could it talk, they would question it later.

Wikkell stood glaring down at the giant worm, his breath still coming fast from his exertions. "Call off your bats!" he ordered the coiled creature.

Deek uncoiled slightly and scraped part of himself over the rock beneath his body. "H-h-have y-your W-whites c-c-cease t-their d-d-destruction!"

Cyclops and worm glared at each other.

"You have allowed them to get away!"

"I-I h-have a-allowed it? I-it is y-y-you w-who a-allowed it!"

Behind Wikkell, one of the Whites screamed, struggling with three bats who had stuck their feeding tubes into him.

"While we stand here arguing, they move further into the tunnels. Perhaps we can strike a bargain? We can work together. There are three of them, after all; we can divide them up when we catch them. They all look alike . . . who is to know?"

Deek considered this for a moment. Aye, better to have One Eye where he could be seen, and there was some merit in the plan, not that he intended to share anything once the men were collected. "A-a-agreed!"

Wikkell held his smile in check. Once they caught the humans, he could smash the worm with a big rock and that would be the end of it. In the meantime, it would be better to have the witch's thrall where he could keep his eye watching it.

"Let us go, then," Wikkell said.

"W-wh-what of y-your W-w-whites?"

Wikkell turned to look. Most of the Whites were down; a few still hurled rocks at the swooping fliers.

"Let the bats have them; thus far they have only gotten in my way."

"A-as h-have the b-b-bats. C-c-come."

Deek moved quickly, but with added caution. He trusted One Eye less than the distance he could fly like a bat, which was to say, not at all.

Together, cyclops and worm started for the tunnel.

In his chamber, Rey's impatience simmered to a roiling bubble.

In her bed, Chuntha's agitation at being kept waiting blossomed like a bitter fungus.

"Which way?" Conan asked as the three fleeing humans came to a triple forking of tunnels.

Tull scratched at his beard. "I dunno," he said. "I never took this route afore."

"One is as good as another," Elashi said. "The center path."

Before either man could speak, the desert woman

hurried into the chosen tunnel. Tull raised a questioning eyebrow at Conan.

Conan shrugged. "She is like that. I have found it better not to argue. It saves much time."

The two men followed Elashi.

"Best you slow down," Conan called to Elashi. She was perhaps ten spans ahead of the Cimmerian youth and running nearly full out.

"Can't keep up, Conan?" she called back.

"No, it is just that—"

His words were interrupted by Elashi's scream. She dropped suddenly from view, and her disappearance was followed almost immediately by a splash. Conan increased his speed and skidded to a halt on the damp rock just short of where the desert woman had vanished.

He found himself on the edge of the largest cavern yet, balanced on a rocky lip overlooking a vast lake; he could not see the far shore as the fungal glow faded rapidly with distance, the water being illuminated only by the roof, a good ten spans above.

A span or so below Conan, Elashi came up from the water, which reached only to her hips. Conan grinned down at her. "I can keep up. It is just that we don't know these tunnels and we might happen upon something unexpected," he said.

"I hate you!" Elashi said.

Tull slid to a stop next to Conan, overbalanced and nearly fell but was stopped by an outthrust brawny arm.

"Take care," Conan said.

Tull nodded, regaining his breath. "The Sunless Sea."

"You know this place?"

"I have seen it from a different vantage point, but yes." To Elashi, Tull said, "Best you exit the water, lass. There are certain creatures who live in it—"

Whatever ending Tull intended to his sentence was lost in the splashing Elashi made as she frantically left the water. To Conan's left was a kind of beach a few steps away, and it was but four heartbeats before Elashi attained this drier vantage point. A short ledge led from the mouth of the tunnel along the rock wall to the beach, and Conan and Tull made their way down to the shore to join the woman.

Elashi began to remove her wet clothing, wringing it out as she did so.

"Give me your cape," she said to Conan, who managed to keep himself from smiling as he tendered the garment. The fall had served her right, but it was probably best to refrain from speaking it thus. She wrapped herself in the cape, which was hardly drier than her own clothing.

"So," Conan said, "what of this sea?"

"I know only a little about it," Tull answered. "It widens as you see here, and narrows to a small river's width in other places. S'posed to go on for miles and miles, though it's more like a large lake 'n a true sea—the water ain't brine. I learned this from a White I captured once."

"Go on."

"No one knows for certain where the sea ends, but it might be that it eventually emerges above the ground."

Conan looked at the still water. "That would be reason enough to follow it."

"Had we but a ship and rowers," Elashi put in. Sarcastically, as usual.

"That might be possible," Tull said. "After a fashion."

"How so?" Conan asked.

"There are creatures in the water. A form of giant whiskered fish is among them. As big as a house, if the White could be believed."

"So?"

"In my youth I fished the great western rivers," Tull said. "These bottom fish contain large bladders filled with air. When the creatures die, they will float for a time. With one of them, we might make a raft. We could use fins and large bones as paddles."

"All well and good," Elashi said, "but how are we to collect this monster fish?"

"We have your swords and my knife," Tull said. "A sure stroke in a vulnerable spot would slay one."

"And what is to draw one of these fish to a place where we could slay it?" she continued. "We have no bait."

Conan and Tull glanced at each other, then back at Elashi. The two men grinned.

Whatever else the desert woman was, she was not slow of wit. "Ha! You are both mad!"

"The other choice is to stay here forever and face the worms, bats, Whites and cyclops," Conan said, "not to mention the wizard and the witch."

"Then one of *you* may act as bait!"

Tull said, "I am the fisherman. I must watch for the signs of the creature."

"And I am much better with my blade than are you with yours," Conan said. "Do you think you could slay a fish as large as a house with that needle you carry?"

"I will not do it," Elashi said. "You are both addled completely out of your feeble minds!"

Tull sketched a picture of the fish in the wet sand near the water's edge. "You must drive your blade in here," he said, indicating a spot just behind the head. "Angled in thus, to sever the great nerve within the spine, here."

Conan nodded.

"The flesh is soft, as is the bone, but it will require a powerful stab, likely to the full depth of your blade."

Conan nodded again.

Tull stood and brushed the sand from his hands. "Farther along the shore, just there, is a likely spot. You see that spire of rock that juts out over the water?"

"I see it."

"If the lass swims in the deep water below it, you will be positioned to stab the fish as it passes underneath."

Elashi grinned at this. "Ah, a shame. I would be willing to go along with this moon-mad plan, but alas, I cannot swim a stroke. Ask Conan, he knows. So much for your plan."

"No need to swim," Tull said. "You will dangle from the rock spire. We can cut that cloak into strips for a swing."

"But—but—" she began.

"So much for your objections," Conan said.

It took less than an hour to make everything ready. Elashi hung from the spire, only her feet touching the surface below. Tull had her waving her legs back and forth, agitating the water. Above her, Conan stood with his sword held in both hands, point held down. Tull watched the water in the distance.

"If you allow a fish to eat me, I shall never forgive you, Conan. I will follow you around the Gray Lands for ten thousand years making you regret it, I swear."

Conan considered that thought and found it as unpleasant as any he had ever had. To be tormented by a woman's bitter tongue for eternity, aye, now there was a truly hellish thing. Surely Crom would not punish any man so?

"Look there," Tull said. He pointed.

Conan looked. A wide ripple seemed to be approaching them. "I see no fish."

"But you see the water of its passage. It will have to come closer to the surface as it approaches. In a moment . . . ah, there!"

Something thin and spined broke the surface.

"Its dorsal fin!" Tull cried. "Make ready, lad!" To Elashi he said, "I'll pull you up when it gets close enough."

"You had better!" Elashi said.

"By Mitra, it's a big 'un," Tull said. "You could feed a whole village for an entire moon on it!"

"Should not you pull me up now?"

"A moment more. Conan?"

"I am ready." The Cimmerian took a deep breath, allowed it to escape, and tightened his reverse grip on the sword's handle. Here it came, closer, it was getting closer and closer . . .

"Up we go, lass!" Tull started tugging on the twin ropes of cloth holding Elashi. She came up half a span—

—then the strap on the left broke. The wet *pop!* of the cloth was joined by the woman's scream as she clutched the remaining support, nearly jerking Tull from his perch.

"Mitra's ass!" Tull hollered. He began to pull Elashi upward again. Too slow. The fish would be there in another instant and—

Elashi scrambled up the cloth strand like a monkey, continued past the end Tull held and clambered over him onto his back just as the fish reached the spot where she had dangled.

Screaming a wordless sound, Conan leaped from the spire, landed wide-legged upon the back of the fish, and drove the point of his sword downward with all of his strength. His chest and stomach and shoulders contracted, his arms flexed with power, and the blue iron sank to the hilt in rubbery flesh. He even managed a grin. Why, this was simple.

The fish thrashed, tossing the outlander from its back as a maddened horse would throw a legless rider. Conan hit the water and was battered by sudden waves. The fish's tail slapped the surface next to him as he came up, barely missing him, and the force of the thrashing tail sent the man tumbling through the water like a wood chip in a storm-swollen ditch.

Despite the roiling water, the Cimmerian managed to orient himself and start swimming for the shore. He attained the base of the spire and climbed rapidly, joining Elashi and Tull within a moment.

Beneath the trio, the fish's struggles lessened. Conan's strike had been true. After a few moments the great breast stopped moving on its own. Slowly the dead fish rose to the surface, bobbing up on its side, water streaming downward from scales the size of platters.

Conan grinned at Elashi. "Behold, our boat."

Elashi wrinkled her nose. "It has a loathesome stench already. In a few days it will stink to the ends of the world."

Conan and Tull looked at each other. Some people could find fault everywhere. Give them a chest of gold and they would complain of the weight they must carry.

Eight

"**W**-we h-h-have th-them!" Deek said. He and Wikkell had paused so that the worm could speak: moving and talking at the same time was all but impossible for Deek's kind.

"How so? I see no one here but us."

"Th-this t-t-tunnel l-leads to the S-s-sunless S-sea."

"Ah." Even though Wikkell had spent very little time in this region of the vast Black Cave system, he could not help but know of the sprawling underground lake. "Then they are trapped."

"S-s-so it w-w-would s-s-seem."

"Then let us proceed apace. I feel certain that

80

the two of us can capture and hold a mere three humans."

"W-w-without a d-doubt," Deek agreed.

There were limits to Rey's communication spell. Wikkell was either beyond the reach of the magic or dead, the latter being somewhat more unlikely. Still, either way boded ill for the wizard's plans. If the prey had managed to somehow elude the cyclops and move beyond Rey's range to speak to his servant, that was bad. If Wikkell were somehow indisposed and unable to answer Rey's call, that was also bad. Not for a moment did the magician consider that the cyclops might ignore his hail. So either of the two choices was unacceptable, and yet one of them must indeed be the case.

Katamay Rey moved to a chest of assorted magical impedimenta and began to rummage through it. There was no help for it, then. He would have to gather supplies and a retinue and go find Wikkell, or the barbarian, or both.

Damn. Why was it that anything of consequence always seemed to require his own hand? Did he have to do *every*thing around this place?

Chuntha's patience was ended. That slithering servant of hers was beyond her dreamcasting range, blast him! Who knew what evil might have befallen Deek? The man—the big, strong, handsome, *virile* man—might be escaping her clutches even as she lay upon her bed dreading the very thought.

No. It would not do.

She sighed. She supposed that she should have learned by now not to send a worm to do a witch's job. It had seemed so simple, to merely fetch the man to her—but no, by the Demon Sensha's Hairy Mound, some laughing fate wished to cheat her of her just due. Perhaps the wizard had a hand in it. An unpleasant thought.

Chuntha raised her naked form from the sodden bed and moved to gather a collection of certain items of magical power. Very well. She had not always been a stay-at-home ruler. She would go and fetch the man herself. And if Deek lived and was whole, he would be made to suffer for her extra labors, too.

The blind white thing responded to the Harskeel's questions, speaking in a tongue that sounded like a tortured monkey's wails. Fortunately, one of the Harskeel's men was familiar with a mountain dialect that was similar enough that some sense could be made of the creature's replies.

"I am only interested in the one called 'Conan,' " the Harskeel said. "Ask it about him."

The pikeman did so.

A stream of babble came from the beast.

"M'lord, he says there was a large man and that he and his brothers were sent to fetch him."

"Ask it who sent it."

More gratings upon the ear.

"He says he works for the one-eyed monster, who in turn works for the wizard of the caves."

The Harskeel shook its head. Treading on a wizard was bad business. There was no help for it, though.

When they had obtained as much information as the Harskeel thought itself apt to get from the white thing, it drew its sword and snapped a quick but powerful cut at the creature's neck. Razor steel met flesh, and the startled cry died even as it was born. The severed head fell, trailing blood, and bounced along the cave floor.

So much for that.

Leading its remaining men, the Harskeel moved off.

Using his sword and Tull's knife, Conan hewed several shallow compartments and numerous footsteps into the flesh of the dead fish. A pair of riblike bones, each fastened to portions of fin with strings cut from his former cape, made passable paddles with which to propel the once-living raft. He also cut some of the fish's flesh into small chunks for eating, though in truth the raw fish held little appeal to his or Elashi's appetite.

"Here," Tull said. "Watch."

With that, the ragged man clambered down from the fish's side—now the top of their raft—and splashed onto the nearest shore. After a moment he returned with a yellowish mushroom he had found at the base of the cave wall. Then he picked up a hand-sized slab of the cut fish and squeezed the fungus over it. Juice from the fungus fell upon the translucent fish, and as it did, the flesh became opaque.

Conan's keen nose noted an acidic tang to the juice, and he remarked upon it.

"Aye," Tull said. "The juice of this particular toadstool is harmless, but it 'cooks' the fish. In a few minutes it'll be like we roasted it in an oven."

Conan was somewhat dubious as to the powers

of toadstool liquid, but a taste of the fish when Tull indicated that it was "done" put an end to his doubts. The fish was delicious! Given that it was the first meal he and Elashi had enjoyed in some time, they ate with gluttonous relish, stuffing the fish down in great mouthfuls.

Somewhat later, feeling sated, Conan said, "I suppose it would be too much to ask that another of these fungi along the wall would serve as wine?"

Tull chuckled. "Would that it were so, lad, but nay. There is a kind of mushroom I've seen that gives visions when eaten, but it has a nasty flavor and is just as apt to make a man puke as dream."

"Thank you, no," Conan said.

Elashi had climbed down the steps Conan had carved into the monster fish and was washing her hands in the water. She finished the chore quickly, mindful of the kind of things Tull had spoken of as living in the lake.

"Well," she said as she ascended the fish back to the shallow depression where Conan and Tull sat digesting their recent meal. "Are we ready to begin this altogether unusual voyage?"

Conan nodded, stood, and stretched. "Aye, and why not?" Joints and sinews popped as he rolled his shoulders and swung his arms back and forth to loosen them.

With that, he fetched one of the paddles. Tull took the other, and they moved to the edges of their fishy boat to stand in the wells they had carved out for support. The Cimmerian looked across the fish at Tull, who nodded, and both men dug their paddles into the water.

Slowly, ponderously, the dead fish began to move.

*   *   *

It was not the best of all possible craft, but once moving, the fish slid through the still water fairly easily. Currents, if there were any, did not seem to impede their progress, and nothing from the depths rose to challenge them.

Not long after they started, the place from whence they had begun their voyage was lost in the darkness. The cave roof oft dipped lower and raised higher, and the side walls were sometimes not in view. It might almost be a lake above ground on a moonlit night, save that the light here was decidedly green and no breath of wind nor insect's call disturbed the silence. There were only the sounds of their paddles splashing in the water and an occasional intestinal groan from the innards of the decomposing fish.

Conan had been in places he preferred more, but all in all, his fortunes could have been considerably worse. He had good companions, a full belly, and control of his movements. His blade was sharp in its sheath, and there would certainly be no lack of food in the foreseeable future. It was true that Crom had not favored him with a gold and gem-encrusted barge, but there was transportation, albeit somewhat slippery, and he and his companions seemed safe from immediate pursuit. Anyone trying to swim after them would likely be apt to find themselves lining the belly of a creature like the one beneath Conan's feet. He found that thought pleasing. A comfortable heat lubricated his shoulders, and the strain of rowing was pleasant, raising a legitimate sweat upon his skin. A man could do far worse.

As to the future? Well, he did not ponder over-much on that. Better to live in the moment and deal with the future when it arrived; elsewise a man might spend his entire life fretting of things that might never come to pass. Such worries would serve only to spend one's alloted time, and were foolish ways to waste it. Even paddling a dead fish over a silent lake, lit by glowing fungus and buried under the earth, certainly bettered the alternative he had been facing only a few hours past. He still lived, and that was the most important fact. Everything else could be worked out as it happened.

Smiling to himself, Conan pulled his paddle through the still water.

"S-s-stand r-r-ready," Deek scraped softly. "H-here is th-the e-e-entrance t-to the s-s-sea."

Wikkell nodded, assuming that whatever passed for eyes on the giant worm could take in the gesture. He flexed his fingers and started forward.

"B-b-be c-c-cautious," Deek warned, "T-th-there s-seems to b-be a d-d-drop a-a-ahead—"

Deek's warning was unnecessary. Wikkell teetered on the brink but kept his balance as he looked over the quiet water below. Quickly he shifted his single-eyed gaze back and forth, taking in the beach and shoreline to the side.

"I see no sign of them."

"I-i-im-p-possible. L-let m-me s-s-see."

Deek undulated to the edge of the tunnel's exit and waved his head back and forth.

"Only a fool would try to swim in that," Wikkell observed. "Could they have a boat?"

"Un-un-unlikely," Deek replied.

"Well, unless they jumped in and drowned, I surmise that they managed some means of transport."

"S-s-so it w-w-would s-seem. L-l-look!"

Wikkell turned his head in the general direction of where he assumed Deek was "pointing." He saw what appeared to be several lengths of short bone and scraps of cloth littering the beach. He moved down the ledge, Deek inching along behind him.

The cyclops' examination of the litter proved his assumption correct. There were piece of cartilaginous, flexible bone, fresh, likely from a fish, and strands of dark, heavy cloth.

"Somehow they have constructed a boat. Out of what, I would dearly like to know, by Set's Black Scales!"

Deek moved from the sand and crumbled rock beach to a more solid surface nearby so that he could address the problem. "W-w-we n-need t-t-transport-t-tation."

"Indeed." Wikkell swept his gaze over the area. "Unfortunately, I see nothing useful for that purpose."

"T-that t-t-tunnel, t-to y-your r-r-right."

"Don't tell me you have a barge hidden in there, Deek."

"N-n-nay. B-but s-some of th-the W-w-webspinners l-live d-d-down th-that w-way."

"How do you know this? And what good does that do us, in any event?"

"I a-am g-g-gifted w-with an ex-excellent sense of s-s-smell. And th-the s-s-spinners c-can m-make almost a-a-anything w-with th-their w-w-webbing."

Wikkell blinked. What a clever thought. Who

would have even expected such from a worm? "Ah, excellent, Deek! You are proving to be a most resourceful traveling companion."

Had Deek a proper mouth, he would have smiled. True, Wikkell the one-eye was one of the wizard's minions, but the compliment sat well in any event. These cyclopes were apparently brighter than they appeared, to so quickly recognize talent in others and to then voice it in such a straightforward manner. Too bad they worked for the wizard. Just as it was too bad that he had to work for Chuntha.

"Let us go and see if we can bargain with the Webspinners."

"I-i-indeed."

Katamay Rey decided to travel light. Aside from two chests full of magical apparatus—scrying crystals, sleezewart, anthelmintics, sleepdust, and assorted spellbooks—he carried only enough food, clothing, and niceties to sustain a dozen men for six weeks. His retinue—a mere score of hunchbacked cyclopes—spread these items of cargo amongst themselves without question. Rey had little appreciation for the intelligence of his thralls, feeling certain that seldom, if ever, there existed a thought in any of their heads that was not an autochthonous one, so placed there by himself. "Stupid" was too kind a term even for the brightest among the cyclopes, Rey figured, and when he laid his gaze upon Wikkell, whom he had considered somewhat promising, that unworthy soul would find himself sorry to have been born.

There was a sedan chair, borne by a pair of stalwarts, but he waved it away. He would walk on his own for a time—a novel idea—and stretch his legs. It had been so long since he had done any exercise, it would be refreshing.

Striding purposefully ahead of the cyclopes, the wizard marched off to attend to business.

Chuntha's saddle was cinched into place on the back of one of the larger worms, a torpid-thinking vermis called Soriusu. Behind her mount, two dozen more of the giant worms twitched, awaiting the witch's command to move. Chuntha's saddle-bags, made from fresh Blind White leather, rested in front of her spread legs. Her erotics, potions, dreaming jewels, and assorted wands lay within, and thin bags of hallucinogenic spore powder nestled along the edge of her saddle within easy reach. She was ready.

"Go!" Chuntha commanded.

Here at the exit to her personal chamber, the light-emitting fungus was particularly strong, and her naked skin, warmed as always by her inner fires, glowed viridly as she moved under the verdant glow. Chuntha smiled to herself. This would be a great adventure, ending in what she was certain would turn out to be a magnificent copulatory episode.

The delicious thought warmed her even more.

Nine

Conan, Elashi, and Tull floated along the Sunless Sea for the best part of a day without major incident. Things did sometimes swirl in the waters around them, sending ripples or an occasional splash their way, but Conan's keen eyes found no source for these actions. Once something large bumped the raft fish from underneath, rocking the three riders, but whatever it was, it troubled them only the one time. Perhaps it had taken a mouthful of their boat and been satisfied.

Near what Conan judged to be evening—who could tell in this land of eternally glowing walls? —they paddled the raft into a quiet cove and wedged it against a rocky shore. It was darker here than in many other places, the light-fungus being rather scantly distributed along the walls of the cove's grotto, and if anybody or anything happened to pass by upon the water, it might well be that they would miss seeing the trio and their make-do boat.

All three of the voyagers were covered with a sticky and smelly fish effluvia, and none had any desire to sleep upon the dead creature could it be avoided. A series of ledges stair-stepped its way up the wall away from the water, and a particularly wide one was an easy two minutes' climb. Perched here, the three shared more of the "cooked" fish. Tull gathered some lichen that was edible, if not deliciously so, and they also chewed on that as they rested.

"I wish we could build a fire," Elashi said. "It is so damp in here."

Conan glanced at the woman, but said nothing.

"I know, I know," she said. "Might as well wish for a kingdom. It was only a thought."

"How far do you reckon we come?" Tull asked.

Conan shrugged. "Miles. Hard to say on the water."

"Aye. Reckon we lost any followers. Kinda hard to track in water."

Conan chewed on a mouthful of the lichen. It had a sour taste but was a change from the fish. Earlier in the day the fish had been the best food he had eaten in a long time; after consuming the pale, bloodless flesh several times since, it had lost much of its appeal.

Likely Tull was right about pursuers, but he would sleep with one hand on his sword. This place was run by a wizard and a witch, and although his experience with magic was slim, he wanted no more part of it. Such things were dangerous and unclean. Give him a fanged beast to face, or berserker swordsmen, and he could hold his own as well as any man. Some spell-spewing necromancer was another thing altogether. Honest men stayed away from such things, and Conan wanted no truck with wizards or witches or any of their ilk.

"I'll stand the first watch," Tull said.

Conan nodded. He looked at Elashi. "We have no fire, but we can share our own warmth."

"Aye," she said, smiling.

The pair of them found a particularly dark recess on the ledge, leaving Tull sitting near the edge, watching the ice-smooth Sunless Sea.

The Webspinner Plants could not move from their rooted position, but they were none the less dangerous for that. The plants, each twice the height of a tall cyclops, with thorny branches surrounding a central maw, produced a spiderlike silk webbing with which they snared their prey. Unlike spiders, most of whom built nets upon which they might catch a hapless passerby, the Webspinner Plants could throw sticky, ropelike lines for some distance. These lines would adhere to anything save the plants' own webbing. The victim thus caught would then be hauled inexorably to the plant, where it would be impaled upon the sharp spikes until it ceased struggling, then drawn into the waiting maw. Around the plants was an artificed floor of shimmery silk-overlay that kept the prey lines from sticking to the cavern's rocky surface. The undigested and regurgitated bones of a thousand meals past lay upon the silken floor, and one desiring to speak to the plants stayed outside the range of the prey lines or took his chances on becoming dinner.

Wikkell and Deek kept well outside the perimeter of the largest of the silk floorings, talking to the queen of this particular nest of Webspinners. Logic dictated that the Webspinners should have been long extinct since they were immobile, and despite their ability to heave lines; any prey species with half a brain should certainly have learned over the years to stay well away from the plants.

However, the Webspinners had another talent, and while both Wikkell and Deek had spoken to them a number of times, that talent was once again in full evidence: the voices of the plants were *most* compelling. What Wikkell heard when the queen spoke was the voice of a female cyclops, honey-smooth and filled with promise of all manner of conjugal delights, almost irresistibly offered. Almost. Deek's hearing apparatus, upon receipt of the same voice, construed the sound as that of a female of his species, gravid with a thousand eggs and desiring a big, strong worm such as himself to fertilize them at his earliest pleasure. Guaranteed pleasure, vermis-mine . . .

Both cyclops and worm knew that the voice was specific to whatever kind of creature that heard it: males heard females and females heard males, generally, and only those with strong minds or experience with the plants could resist the siren song they sang.

"Come closer," the queen of the plants urged, "that we might discuss this without having to strain ourselves by yelling." Surely no cyclopian female had ever sounded so sweet and so willing to do anything Wikkell might desire. Anything at all, would he simply come a bit closer . . .

"Nay, sister," Wikkell said. His voice held no rancor; he understood the mechanisms the plants used and begrudged them not, for everybody wanted to survive. "What we wish to discuss involves a long-term arrangement rather than a quick meal upon Deek here or myself."

"Long term?" Deek heard the gravid female's soothing tones in the high pitch that his kind used, sounds quite inaudible to human or cyclopian ears but hot music to his own. Even knowing what she was, the call tempted him.

"Aye," Wikkell continued. "A large supply of food, spaced over a long period."

"How much? Over how long?" The sweet tones vanished abruptly and the queen's suddenly alien rasp held no promise of anything either Wikkell or Deek or anything interested in staying alive would find intriguing. The big plant was now all business.

Wikkell spared a quick grin and whisper for Deek. "That got her attention."

Softly, Deek scraped back, "I-i-indeed."

Louder, Wikkell said, "We need water transportation. You can spin a boat of your webbing, can you not?"

"Certainly," came her reply. The tone was full of arrogance and disdain. "There is little we cannot create of the Magic Cord."

"In return for supplying my friend Deek and me

with such a conveyance, we would be willing to offer you, oh, say half a dozen each of Whites and bats to be placed within range of your . . . ah . . . supply lines."

"Twenty each," the queen said. "And your boat shall be a thing crafted with the utmost loving care."

Wikkell grinned down at Deek. He whispered, "I think we can bargain her down to half that."

"W-whatever. B-be q-q-quick t-though."

Wikkell addressed the queen again. "The boat need merely float, my leafy queen, not win a contest of beauty. Eight each."

"Even so, such labor requires much skill, mobile one. Sixteen."

In the end they settled on a dozen bats and ten Whites as the price for the craft. To be delivered as soon as Wikkell and Deek finished a small errand they had to accomplish. The queen would rather have eaten something immediately of course, but she knew a good bargain when she had one, and she and her sisters could survive for a long while without eating did they need to.

"Would this errand have anything to do with three small mobile ones who float upon the waters?"

Wikkell blinked his great eye. "You know of them, Majesty?"

"I can speak to all of my sisters via the deep roots we share. The three move away from here, toward the Great Ambit Cave."

"Ah. Well, yes, as it happens, those are the ones we seek."

"If my sisters and I should help you snare these, might not there be an additional price tendered for such a service? We are not all planted here, you know."

Wikkell and Deek regarded each other. They had been given great leeway by their master and mistress, respectively, and they had used more time than originally intended. To fail was to die. "Indeed, Your Majesty. Something could certainly be arranged in that direction."

"Another two dozen each, white walkers and dark fliers," the queen said.

Wikkell grinned. He loved to bargain, and had little chance to do so. "Two dozen? For a mere three? I had thought to offer, oh, say five each."

Even as the smiling cyclops and giant webspinning queen continued their deal, the other plants began spinning an oval, watertight bowl large enough to hold a dozen men.

The night passed quietly for Conan and his friends. He relieved Tull after a few hours, and Elashi chose to sit with him as the older man fell into slumber. She and Conan did not spend all of their time watching the water; indeed, a portion of that evening found them far more intent on each other, and the pleasure thereby derived was both refreshing and tiring at the same time.

In the morning—for lack of a better term—the three remounted the dead fish and paddled away.

Perhaps two hours later, the walls of the cave narrowed considerably, so that the overhanging ledges on both sides could very nearly be touched with one of the paddles. They continued onward with such surroundings for another ten minutes; then the cavern expanded again to thrice larger proportions. Just ahead, however, the waters split in twain as a bifurcation appeared in the rock. One river ran to the left, another of equal size went to the right.

"Which way?" Tull called as he paddled.

"One is as good as the other," Conan replied. "To the right."

Elashi looked agitated at this. Conan refrained from smiling. He had a sudden revelation. "You would rather we went the other way?"

"Did I say that?" she asked.

"No. To the right, then."

"It looks darker that way."

"To the left, then," Conan said, playing his hunch.

"It looks narrower that way," she said.

Conan grinned to himself. He was, he realized, finally beginning to understand how her mind worked. She did not want to make a decision, but she would almost always oppose any that he made. Therefore, to go to the left, he must be adamant about going the other way.

"The right fork is definitely the better way to go," he said. He waited for a heartbeat, and was not disappointed.

"I think it would be better to travel the other fork," Elashi said.

Ah, ha! He was right. But the trick lay in not agreeing too readily. He had to agree without seeming to agree. Complex creatures, women; they would rather argue than do almost anything else.

Conan shrugged. "Very well. I think the right branch would be better, but perhaps you are correct."

"Of course I am."

He turned his head away so she would not see him smile. It worked, this time. Of course one snowflake did not a blizzard make, but at least it was a beginning. Perhaps he might come to understand the ways of women after all.

They paddled the fish into the left branch of the split.

The Harskeel was more than a little tired and much more than a little irritated. What should have taken but a short while had turned into a major imbroglio. All these sundry beasts darting and flittering about to obscure what should be a simple quest. It did not ask for much, the Harskeel— merely to be less than the sum of its parts once again. Was that too much? One brave man and his sword was small compensation for the reversal of its unnatural joining; why could not the fates and the gods tender such a miniscule request? But no. Nothing, nothing, *nothing* was ever easy. Instead of a clean capture and subsequent sundering back into its natural and rightful selves, the Harskeel was forced to grub around under the ground like some ilysiidaen snake! It was all too much.

Well, when it finally captured this Conan fellow, the man would be made to know some of the Harskeel's own torment. After the sword was blooded, perhaps some slow torture would repay the barbarian for the effort expended to retrieve him.

It seemed only fair.

The Harskeel's tracker returned. "We found a tunnel that goes around that bat cave and gets us back on the trail again, m'lord."

"Good. Let us move foward. Mind you keep your pikes at the ready." This last command was hardly needed as the four remaining men had yet to lower their weapons since the slaughter in the bat cave; still, a leader had to remind its followers who did what every now and again.

The Harskeel smoothed an eyebrow and patted its hair,—somewhat to its own disgust, as well as a sense of rightness—and followed the tracker along the new trail.

Rey now rode in the sedan chair, rocking comfortably with the walking rhythm of its two bearers. The wizard looked around. It had been too long since he had ventured out to observe his domain, far too long. What was the point in ruling if one could not go out and lord it over the realm now and then? He resolved that once this man was dispatched to the Gray Lands and That Bitch dealt her just reward, he would get out more often.

The drone of the marching cyclopes, keeping step together, lulled the wizard into a comfortable somnambulance. He leaned back against the chair, his head lolling to one side as he dozed and daydreamed of future glories.

The undulations of the worm clasped within her spread thighs gently shifted Chuntha back and forth like a waving frond in an alternating breeze. The rasp of belly plates over the damp rock was almost melodic: *scrape, scr-a-a-p-e*—a short beat followed by a longer one as the coils slid the creature forward. A pleasant way to travel, although she could easily think of several ways that would increase the pleasure. But another time; the stalemate between herself and the wizard needed to be put to rest; that concerned her now more than her immediate pleasure. Settle with him once and for all. After that she could perhaps expand her activities to take in a portion of the world above the caves. A more ready supply of men existed there, of course, and one could never have too many of them around. They went so fast.

Rocking with pleasure, Chuntha dreamed of future glories.

Ten

The silken vessel was most interesting, Deek and Wikkell agreed. It was light enough for Wikkell to lift with one hand, and yet banging it accidentally against a wall produced no apparent damage. The craft would easily hold them and perhaps two more passengers as large as they, and the plants had thoughtfully provided a floor inside for added support and comfort.

Once the cyclops and worm reached the sea, the wondrous boat rode high in the water with nary a leak. Utilizing a large sculling oar produced by the plants—at no extra charge—Wikkell saw Deek safely aboard, locked the oar into place, then hopped into the vessel and rapidly propelled the boat away from the shore.

While Deek had no hands, he was able to use the tip of his tail to assist Wikkell with the sculling. The gleaming, silvery craft sped over the smooth water at a pace both occupants found quite amazing.

"I doubt that I could run this quickly," Wikkell observed.

Deek made no audible reply, the bottom of the boat being too smooth for his vocal apparatus to engage, but he was of a like mind. The plants built well, no arguing that. Something to keep in mind for the future. One could construct a number of things from this remarkable webbing.

"Surely the prey we pursue cannot travel half so fast," Wikkell said. "We should catch them in short order."

If we do not take a wrong turning, Deek thought.

"That is, if we do not take a wrong turning," Wikkell said. "But we have help from the plants, after all."

Deek could not speak but he lifted his head and waved it up and down in a gesture that he hoped would pass for a nod.

Wikkell caught the motion and smiled, showing his square and sturdy teeth. "Yes, indeed. I begin to have hopes that this venture might well turn out in our favor after all, Deek old son."

Deek nodded again. The boat skimmed along the water, carrying them after their quarry. Perhaps, Deek thought, he might yet escape the lime pits and come out of this with some kind of victory. A shame he was going to have to flatten Wikkell, though. He was beginning to grow fond of the cyclops. Perhaps there was another way to get the people without killing his new friend. He could explore that idea, certainly; it was the least he could do.

A single cruising bat spied the Harskeel's man sitting alone on the rock next to the sea, and apparently decided that such a meal was simply too good to bypass. The bat dived, already extruding his pointed feeding tube to skewer the unsuspecting delicacy.

Unfortunately for the bat, the man was not alone, and merely acting as bait for just such an attack. The flying rodent had no sooner lit upon the man than he was set upon and captured by three other men who had lain hidden nearby, under the direction of the Harskeel. The bat thrashed and fluttered, but the touch of cold and sharp iron at his throat brought the struggle to a fast end.

"I would speak with you," the Harskeel said.

The bat made no reply.

"Ah, you do not understand civilized speech. A pity. Kill it," the Harskeel ordered.

"Wait!" the bat called out. His voice was high and the accent made the word almost unintelligible, but the Harskeel grinned at the sound of it.

"Hold," it commanded.

The Harskeel's men stayed their pikes.

"Now," the Harskeel said, "how are you called?"

The bat gnashed sharp teeth. When he spoke, his voice was haughty. "I am Crimson So Strong, High Flier and Drinker of Life."

"Crimson?"

"Named for the beautiful splash of that same color upon the fur of my back."

"Fine. 'Red' will do for a name. Now, Red, I have a proposition for you."

"A proposition? We do not deal with those who hold us captive."

"Let him go."

The Harskeel's men released the bat, who gathered himself for a fast escape.

"Before you leave, Red, you should at least hear my proposition. Not that I think you shall get very far, you understand. Zate over there can skewer you before you rise more than this high." The Harskeel held up its thumb and forefinger, separated by the thickness of a boot heel.

Red turned slightly to look at the man called Zate. That worthy grinned brightly and hefted his pike meaningfully.

"I was merely stretching my cramped wings," Red observed. "Certainly I should be most interested to hear your proposition."

"Your kind drinks blood for sustenance, do they not?"

"I feel that you already know that," Red answered.

"As it happens, I have dabbled in magic now and again," the Harskeel said.

Behind the Harskeel, one of its men snickered. The Harskeel did not pause, nor did it turn. As soon as all of this was done, that man was as good as dead, one could bet one's fortune on that.

The Harskeel continued smoothly. "And, as it also happens, I am in possession of a spell that will produce fresh blood in a large quantity."

"You jest," Red said. "You are pulling my wing."

"Perhaps a sample for your edification?"

With that, the Harskeel produced a small brass

bowl from its purse and held it out for the bat to inspect. Red took the bowl and looked at it carefully. "This is empty," the bat said. He rapped a knuckle against the metal, producing a hollow clink. "I see no blood."

The Harskeel retrieved the bowl. "I wished you to be assured there was no trickery involved." The Harskeel pushed its shirt-sleeves back, showing its arms to be bare, and held the small brass bowl cupped in its hands. It began to speak quietly in a language that it knew none around it could understand.

The Harskeel finished its incantation.

The bowl began to fill. Dark liquid welled quickly, reaching the brim of the bowl and forming a meniscus. The Harskeel handed the bowl to Red, who sniffed it.

"Why, it smells just like—"

"—blood," the Harskeel finished. "Go ahead, taste it."

Red looked at the blood and his feeding tube started to flick out, then stopped. "How do I know it is not poisoned?"

The Harskeel smiled. "You do not. However, why should I bother? If I had wanted you dead, I could have easily had you impaled upon three pikes earlier."

Red considered this. "That makes good sense." He extruded his feeding tube and inserted it into the bowl of liquid. Faster than it had come, the blood vanished.

"Why, this is excellent! The best I have ever tasted!"

"So glad you liked it."

"This spell, what would it take to obtain it? And how much of this nectar can it produce?"

"I thought you might get to that. The spell has limits, of course. You might get as much as, oh, six or seven barrels."

"Seven *barrels?* How . . . how wonderful! We could feast a hundred of us on that."

"Of course the spell will recharge itself after a few days, and be able to make that much more each time."

"I must have it! Ask anything!"

The Harskeel grinned. Truly these bats were not adept at trading. In fact, the spell would produce a half dozen barrels of blood, but only once. Were this fluid not consumed rapidly, it would clot within a matter of hours, making it totally useless. Of course by the time the bats found that out, the Harskeel planned to be long gone.

"I am following someone who escaped via this body of water," the Harskeel said. "I require a boat, and someone who can tow it as well."

"That's all?"

"I am a generous sort."

Red glanced at the empty bowl. "Well, I must confess that there is little free wood in the caves. Boats are normally made from wood."

"I care not if the craft is made from dung, so long as it floats."

"Hmm. I am certain that we can come up with what you require. I shall convey this offer to my brothers and we will most assuredly manage something. You, ah, will wait right here until I return?"

"Indeed I shall."

"I shall hurry." Red gathered himself to leap

into flight, then paused. "You might want to tell Zate to stay his pike."

The Harskeel laughed. "No problem, Red, my friend."

With that, the bat zipped into the air and darted away.

The Harskeel watched the bat flit off through the nearest exit. It was very pleased with itself. A small spell that would buy him the barbarian's capture was cheap enough. If all of the bats were as gullible as Red, the transaction would be as smooth as a looking glass. They could be easily bluffed and tricked; Zate's skill with a pike, for instance, was such that he would be most lucky to hit a man-sized target at two paces, much less a flying bat at five times that distance. Pikes were not meant to be thrown; it would take a stronger man than Zate to manage such a task.

"This river seems to go on forever," Elashi said.

"Aye," Conan responded. "And it seems also to be curving to our right."

"Best hope we come to a stopping point soon," Tull said. "Look."

Conan and Elashi followed the direction of Tull's pointing finger. Conan saw what the man meant immediately, although Elashi did not. "What?" she asked. "I see nothing amiss."

"The fish rides lower in the water," Conan said. "Observe the 'steps' I cut out."

Indeed, it was obvious that their boat was sinking, albeit slowly; several of the steps nearest the edges of the great fish were under the water.

"Why is it doing that?" Elashi asked.

Conan shrugged. He knew little of such things.

Tull said, "Perhaps other fishy predators were at the bottom during the night. Or perhaps our mount is becoming waterlogged."

"Can we do anything about it?"

"Find a good spot to start walking, I should think," Tull said. "Although we can probably get another day or two out of it before it goes under for good."

An hour later Conan shook his head. "I like this not," he said.

"What now?" Elashi asked.

"We have turned almost back in the same direction whence we came."

"I see no signs of that. How can you know this?"

Conan shrugged again. He had an innate sense of direction, had had it as long as he could remember. It was possible for him to get lost, of course, but some inner guide usually oriented him quickly, no matter what the surroundings.

"Well, it does not really matter, does it? Anyone following us will have to take the same waterway. So it loops and twists a bit, so much the better—we shall be harder to find and see for that."

Conan did not speak to this. Perhaps Elashi was right. He had no logical reason to feel trepidatious; still, some atavistic sense stirred within him, and he prepared himself for the worst.

Rey was surprised as he entered the breeding cave of the Bloodbats: the place was virtually empty. Well, of living things, in any event. The floor showed signs of a fairly active stour: the dessicated bodies of several Blind Whites and men lay strewn carelessly about, as well as a number of slain bats. Hmm. It seemed that his prey had passed this way. But . . . where were the bats who normally clung to the walls and ceilings? There were only a few of them dead upon the floor, and the wizard could not imagine the remainder abandoning their cave over such trifles. A little blood never bothered the bats.

Rey laughed, amused by his own joke. Blood did not bother the bats. That was a good jest! He would have spoken it aloud, but he realized that his escort of cyclopes would likely see little humor in it. Stupid creatures, one and all, and fit only for thralls.

Yes, well, that was all fine and good, but he had business to which he must attend. The bats had obviously gotten off somewhere to do something, and he would likely discover that purpose eventually. Besides, that was not the primary reason for his trip by any means. No, and the presence in the cave of dead men other than those he sought did not seem a benevolent augury. One had to wonder who they were and how they had gotten here, and in what way were they connected to the ones Rey sought. That a connection existed he doubted not at all. He had not lived as long as he had by trusting coincidence any farther than he could pitch a cyclops one handedly.

Rey waved, and the pair of cyclopian chair-carriers bent and lifted his sedan from the ground. Well, he would get to the root of it soon enough.

In that grating-over-rock voice her thralls had, the advance worm returned to tell Chuntha of the carnage in the bats' breeding cave. That news did not bother the witch a whit, but the worm also bespoke a more unpleasant fact: the wizard had moved through the cave, along with a number of one-eyes carrying large amounts of cargo.

Chuntha shifted uneasily on the worm she rode. This boded ill. Something was definitely out of order in the caves if that sluglike wizard would bother to stir his indolent self and go venturing about. That he wanted to steal her barbarian she knew; the lengths to which he would go to thwart her surprised her somewhat.

The witch's resolve hardened. So be it. If the wizard wanted a fight, fine. She would give it to him. She was no fragile wisp to be blown away by his hot air. She would see about this!

Her mount responded to the pressure of Chuntha's knees and began his segmented glide once again. The other worms initiated their own crawls, and the party moved on.

Perhaps two-score bats arrived at the Harskeel's location, dragging by lines behind them what appeared to be several large wooden doors.

The bat named Red flitted down to stand before the Harskeel. "Your boat," he said.

The Harskeel observed the ancient planking. "You call these things a boat?"

The bat shrugged. "You said it need merely float."

"It must also hold my weight and that of my men."

"If it does not, no matter. We shall fly above and support the difference as we tow the thing."

The Harskeel considered that. In point of fact, it

had little choice, were it to continue its pursuit of Conan and his companions. With the bats towing the "boat," surely they would make good speed. "Very well," the Harskeel said. "Let us assemble it and make ready to depart."

Red smiled, showing his needle-pointed teeth. "We would fly much faster were we not so hungry."

The Harskeel grinned. So, the creatures were not quite as trusting as he had at first thought. Ah, well. No matter. "Have you a container?"

"As it happens, there is a depression in the rock, just over there." Red pointed with a wing tip. "The cleft at the bottom of the declivity should hold about a barrel's worth of liquid, if I am any judge of such things."

"When it comes to liquid, I bow to your expertise," the Harskeel said. "Come, then, and allow me to offer you some nourishment."

The bats flocked around the Harskeel as it filled a hole in the rock with blood. After they had finished drinking, all of the bats agreed that it was quite the best-quality meal they had ever had. Promises from the witch and wizard meant nothing compared to this, they said. They were the Harskeel's friends forever!

"Tell me more about this witch and wizard," the Harskeel said.

Gladly, the bats replied. Anything for such a fine friend. Anything at all.

Eleven

The passage in which the three steered the slowly sinking fish narrowed, although Conan could see that it widened considerably up ahead. A few moments later, they attained the wider passage. Almost immediately Conan knew that something was wrong. He glanced around and saw the cause of his worry. Behind them was the mouth of the narrow pass through which they had just emerged. Next to it was a similar opening. Conan stopped his paddling.

"What is it?" Tull asked.

"Observe," Conan said, pointing with the paddle. Tull and Elashi turned to look behind them.

"Uh-oh," Tull said.

"What is the matter?" Elashi asked. "I see nothing but two large holes in a wall. Is there some pursuit?"

Conan said, "Do you not recognize this place? You were set on entering one over the other not so long ago."

Elashi shook her head. "What *are* you babbling about?"

The big Cimmerian nodded at the twin passages behind them. "We have made a loop," he said. "Yesterday we entered that passage on the left. Now we have returned to the same spot. If there is any pursuit, likely it will come from the direction in which we now travel."

"Oh!" Elashi said. "Oh, dread."

Dread indeed, Conan thought. It seemed that there would be no way out of the underground via this waterway.

"What are we to do now?" Elashi asked.

"I think it best we beach this stinking fish corpse and resume our travels on foot," Conan answered. "As I recall, there were a series of small openings on the wall only an hour or so ahead."

Tull said, "Aye, right, lad. Our boat should get us that far."

"The faster, the better," Conan said.

Both men dug their makeshift paddles into the water deeply. The sodden fish moved slowly, but move it did.

Wikkell and Deek paused to dine upon several carefully selected fungi and to rest from their labors at the scull oar. While neither creature was bothered by toadstools that would fatally fell a man, each had his own preference as to flavor, and so each searched for the particular variety of cave-growing fungus that suited him best. They were fortunate in finding their favorites in short order.

"I would say we made excellent time thus far today," Wikkell said around a mouthful of putrid yellow mushroom.

Deek, now firmly upon solid rock, scraped his reply. "I-indeed. A p-p-pleasant w-way to t-t-travel."

Wikkell nodded. "Aye. And I was thinking that the plants might well be able to produce other items that we might find useful. Clothing, per-haps; or they might even be persuaded to manu-facture furniture."

"T-that s-s-same th-th-thought had c-crossed m-my m-mind." Since it was not necessary for Deek to utilize his mouth for speech, he continued to eat all the while he said this.

"Of course we would eventually run out of bats and Whites to trade, but I for one cannot say I would be greatly aggrieved if that should come to pass."

"N-n-nor w-w-would I."

Wikkell swallowed a mouthful of his meal. "By that time, we could have the caves looking very fine indeed." He started to take yet another bite of the mushroom but paused, suddenly remember-ing. "The wizard would never allow it," he said, his voice sad.

Deek paused in his own mastication. "T-t-too r-right. N-n-neither w-would the w-w-witch."

Wikkell's appetite was gone of a moment. He tossed the mushroom aside and brushed the crumbs of it from his lips. "I do not recall it personally, of course, but I am told that the caves were a much happier place before the coming of the wizard and the witch."

"S-s-so I t-too h-have h-h-heard. A p-p-pity."

Wikkell stood and rubbed his hands together to warm them. "Well, there's nothing to be done for it, is there? To raise a hand against Katamay Rey would result in instant liquidity and putrification."

"C-c-chuntha p-prefers the l-l-lime pits."

Both Wikkell and Deek gave out with their versions of a shudder.

"Best we depart, Deek old slug. The sooner we get this business behind us, the better."

"A-a-aye, O-one-Eye. O-one m-m-must d-deal w-with r-r-reality."

"Unfortunately. Come. I shall assist you into our boat."

"Y-y-you are t-too k-k-kind."

After Deek was aboard, Wikkell shoved the lightweight craft into the water and hopped inside. As soon as the oar cleared the shore, he began bending it back and forth in the powerful scull he had gotten better at as they had traveled. Perhaps there was some way he and Deek could both come out of this adventure with their skins whole. There were, after all, at least three humans, and from the debacle he had witnessed in the bat cave, likely a few more loose ones running about. Were Wikkell to return with several of them for Rey's pleasure, who was to know if Deek also captured a few for the witch?

According to the oral history of the caves, there had been a time hundreds of seasons past when the cyclopes and the worms had gotten along together rather well, living in harmony and bothering no one. The plants had feasted upon the much stupider Whites and bats, and life had been an altogether better proposition than it was under the rule of either witch or wizard. Wikkell could see how it might have been so: this Deek was a pleasant enough sort, much better company than a haughty bat or a jibbering moron of a White, and certainly much, much nicer than the human wizard, with his noxious spells and offhand death-dealing. At the very least, Deek considered the cyclopes thinking beings, even if enemies, something Rey could not bring himself to believe. Perhaps there was some way to avoid braining the great worm with a rock after all. Wikkell would think about it and gently broach the subject when it might be appropriate.

All of which was moot, of course, did they not catch the humans, and soon.

Wikkell bent to his oar, thinking of the unpleasant alternative to losing their prey.

Offhand, the Harskeel could not recall ever having traveled or even having heard of anyone who had traveled in such a ridiculous manner. It and its men sat perched upon the damp planks of their "boat," which was being hauled rapidly along an underground waterway by no less than forty blood-drinking bats. Would that he could see such an assemblage passing by from the shore. Surely it must be a sight to behold from that angle.

There was nothing funny, however, in being in competition with both a powerful wizard and an equally powerful witch for the bounty they all sought. The Harskeel had a healthy respect for magic, garnered the hard way, and its only hope was to obtain the prize first and be gone before a bigger dog arrived to take it. The bats, expansive with blood-bloated bellies, had told him all about the wizard and the witch and their enthralled agents, the cyclopes and the giant worms. This proposition grew trickier by the moment.

Still, the Harskeel considered, it was itself not without resources. Aside from its remaining men— not the most adept of warriors, but who would fight well to protect their hides—the Harskeel also had a few small spells of its own. Granted, it was no adept at magic, either, but with the element of surprise on its side, a minor conjure at the right time might well turn the contest in its favor. A blinding light here or a thick fog there could alter the course of a battle. There were five barrels of blood left in the spell he had promised the bats. Said creatures would scarcely appreciate wasting such a delectable treat by having it pour down upon an enemy, but the Harskeel hardly considered the wants of the bats germane to its own plans. One did what one had to do to win, and demons devour the losers.

The makeshift craft skimmed over the water, throwing up a fine spray, such was the thing's bat-augmented speed. As long as they had to deal with only a single worm and one hunchbacked cyclops, it could be managed. Could they but stay ahead of the witch and the wizard, the game was still within the Harskeel's reach. At this speed, it did not see how it could lose.

*   *   *

Once again Rey's temper flared hotter. This was all very amusing, to go forth seeking sport, but he had come to the edge of the Sunless Sea without sighting either his prey or his cyclops. Perhaps Wikkell was dead after all, and if so, just as well, for failure was something Rey could not abide. There were a hundred other cyclopes who could replace Wikkell, though the fool had once shown promise.

Never mind that, Rey thought. By the process of elimination, the man he sought must be somewhere farther along. He must have obtained a boat of some kind. No matter. He would not escape that easily.

Rey called for his chest of spells. The cyclops bearer shambled forth and deposited the case upon the rock. The beast clunked the load down somewhat heavily.

"Careful, fool! Should you break the wrong item, this entire cave could disappear into limbo!"

A lie, of course, but Rey enjoyed the instant look of fear that appeared on the face of the cyclops.

Rey dug around in the case until he found *The Book of Structural Theurgy*. He caused a small flame to burn at the tip of his right thumb so that he might better view the text. He leafed through the pages. Temples, Castles—no, that was too far, back up—Buildings, Bridges. Ah, there it was. Now if his memory served, there should be a spell here . . .

Set's Scales! Where was it? He knew he had used the spell before; it was like a bridge at the shore that appeared in the direction one traveled and disappeared behind. It had to be here somewhere ... wait, it came to him, he should look under "Dock."

Yes. There it was.

Rey mumbled the proper phrases, made the appropriate gesturology, and waited expectantly. A heartbeat later the dock blinked into existence, as solid as could be.

The wizard smiled at the sudden drone of the cyclopes. *That is correct, morons. I am Katamay Rey, your master, and best you never forget it.*

Magic concluded, Rey returned to his sedan and waved one indolent hand toward the dock. "Forward," he said.

His carriers obeyed. Before they reached the end of the magical dock, another section popped into view, extending the dock that much farther into the water. As the party neared the end of that section, yet another appeared, while behind them, the dock next to the shore winked out as if it had never been. The wizard could have caused it to remain, of course, but the cost would have been high. Conservation of magical energy was necessary were one to avoid overextending one's self.

The pace was stately rather than rapid, but Rey did not worry over this. He knew that the Sunless Sea ended some distance ahead in a loop, so sooner or later, anything that traveled that way upon the waters would return in this direction.

It was only a matter of time.

Chuntha's travels led her to a different fjord of the Sunless Sea than that of her rival's. This had been her intent, and she planned to remain behind that bastard of a wizard and out of sight until they came upon the man they both sought. She could not see the wizard ahead, but her scout had returned with news of his position, and he was right where she wanted him. With surprise on her side, she would take care of him once and for all.

The immediate problem was how to navigate the waterway, but a clever witch was never stymied by such trifles.

"All of you, assemble over here," she commanded the worms. "Side by side, in rows, thusly." She gestured, to show the worms the proper ranks.

The creatures came and did as they had been bidden. Eight worms across and three lengthwise they lay, pressed together into a large mat.

From her selection of wands, Chuntha procured a thin rod, no thicker than her middle finger but nearly half her height. Holding this before herself with both hands, she began to rub it over her body, up and down. At the same time, the witch murmured the melodious tones of the spell, a singsong performed in a language from a time when mankind was yet very young.

The casting took effect. She opened her mouth and from it a torrent of fluid emerged, spraying and soaking the ranks of worms as Chuntha walked around and around them. As the liquid touched each worm, it flowed under it, coating it completely. The fluid was sweet-smelling and more volatile than water, and a moment after it covered the creatures beneath the woman, the secretion hardened into a pliable gel.

"Now," Chuntha said, "on my command, the center rank will contract into a half-loop, the front rank will allow itself to be pushed forward, and the rear rank will be dragged along. We are going to inch along to the water. Go!"

To the amazement of the worms, they were now joined together as solidly as if they were one creature. Chuntha smiled as she watched the connected worms move, knowing that they must be thinking she planned to drown them all.

The mat reached the water, and to the further amazement of the leading creatures, it began to float. More, no water came through the gel surrounding them, but air seemed to pass quite freely.

After a few moments, Chuntha had her boat. She loaded her luggage aboard the raftlike construction, first removing from her bags another wand, this one shaped like a wooden screw such as might be used in a fruit press. She placed this to the rear of the raft, where it clung magically. A short incantation and the screw trebled in size, then began to turn. The effect of this worm-gear device was to drive the raft of worms forward.

Chuntha smiled and went to stand at the front of the raft, naked legs spread wide, the gentle breeze of their motion ruffling her hair. She was quite pleased with herself. Quite pleased.

Twelve

Conan's plan to ride their decomposing boat to the tunnels he had earlier seen was not to be. The dead fish, aside from filling the cavern with a noxious, rotting stench, had also begun to sink to the point where it was almost impossible to propel it with the fin paddles Conan and Tull wielded. The cold water of the underground sea washed over the trio's ankles even at the center of the craft.

"Best we attain the shore," Conan said. "There is enough ledge and beach for us to walk. We are not far, as I recall."

"Aye, lad," Tull said. "Good idea."

The two men strained to paddle the hulk closer to shore. Elashi leaped to the rocky outcrop closest to them, followed by Tull and then Conan. The fish bobbed somewhat higher in the water now that it was free of its human riders, but water still covered most of it. As Conan watched, the fish jerked slightly: something must be feeding on it from below.

"This way," Conan said.

He led them up a narrow ledge that wound deeper into the rocks. The wall of the cave was a goodly distance from the water here, and the glow-fungus was scanty on the outcrops, making the footing treacherous in the darkness. Even so, the Cimmerian's sharp eyes managed to spy a relatively safe path.

They were no more than five minutes away from where they had abandoned their boat when Conan stopped and waved Elashi and Tull to silence. He heard something. The sound was difficult to trace due to the surrounding rock and the echoes it cast, but it seemed to be coming from the water.

"Take cover," Conan ordered. "Something approaches on the sea."

Tull and Elashi obeyed, scrunching down behind nearby boulders. Conan himself moved into a patch of heavy shadow next to a fallen stalagtite twice his height and diameter. He squatted and froze into immobility.

After a moment the source of the sound grew nearer and he recognized the noise even as he saw its cause: a boat, with a sculling oarsman whose stroke occasionally broke the surface with a small splash.

And what an oarsman! The creature stood half again Conan's height, bore a large hump upon its

furry back, and had but a single eye. Bald it was,
but with a thick beard. It had massive arms and
squarish, thick fingers, and its movements propelled the boat along at thrice the best speed Conan
and Tull had managed to move the fish.

The boat was silvery, shining almost as if it
were a looking glass upon the darker water, and of
what it was constructed, Conan could not guess.
As the craft drew abreast and rapidly past, Conan's
superior height allowed him to see into the boat.
Lying upon the floor next to the one-eyed giant
was what appeared to be a giant grub. White it
must be, even in the green light, and segmented
like a worm, as big around as a barrel at the
center, and rounded on both ends. Conan wondered if these were the same two he had seen
vaguely in the bats' cave.

The Cimmerian shook his head as the craft and
its strange occupants passed. He wanted no part of
this pair. A few moments later the thing was out of
sight, and Conan moved to where Tull and Elashi
waited.

"Did you see?" Conan asked.

"Aye," Tull answered. "A cyclops and one of the
giant white worms. Odd, though. They're enemies,
on opposite sides. Strange they'd be together. I
never seen 'em that way afore."

"My, how wonderful," Elashi said. "They have
teamed up on our account. You must be proud,
Conan."

"Come," Conan said. "They have missed us, and
by the time they realize it, we can be far gone."

With that, the three started moving again, in the
opposite direction of the cyclops and the worm.

* * *

Deek lifted his head and seemed agitated. Wikkell understood; he knew little about the sensory apparatus of the worms, but did it function at all, it could hardly miss the reek that filled the air. Spoiled fish, and no mistake about it.

"To our right," Wikkell said, "just ahead, there floats the cause of the stink, friend Deek. One of the great fish that inhabit the sea has gone to join its ancestors, so it seems."

Wikkell spared the fish a glance. Quite a large creature, he noted. It must have been most formidable when alive.

Deek raised the front portion of himself up over the edge of the boat and observed the dead fish. Its brother denizens of the depths must have been at it, he saw, for there were great chunks gouged out of the flesh here and there. Something odd about the wounds, though.

Well, the worm thought, it was not their concern. He lowered himself back into the boat and used his tail to once again help Wikkell with the oar.

The openings into the craggy rock wall were easily attained. Tull gathered several clumps of the glow-fungus into a matted ball, in case the tunnels might be devoid of the plant light, and the three ascended the rocky wall and entered the largest of the three openings. Conan felt better almost immediately. There seemed little likelihood of anyone being able to follow them here, not with all of the possible exits from the giant caverns of the Sunless Sea.

Tull's precautions regarding the light seemed sound, as the walls of the new tunnel were mostly dark. The diameter of the tube was perhaps that of a small room, tall enough to stand and walk, but either side being easily reached in a step or two. With Tull holding the ball of fungus high, the three of them started off down the tunnel.

Conan halted suddenly, listening intently.

"What is it?" Elashi asked, her voice a whisper.

Conan strained to hear, but the faint noise he had heard was gone. He shook his head. "Nothing. Let us depart."

They moved off.

The Harskeel's caution in dispatching a scout bat ahead paid dividends. The solitary flier returned and alighted upon the raft. It was Red, and he gave his report gleefully. The three they sought were just ahead! They had entered a tunnel only a few moments' distance. No, they had not seen him, of that Red was certain.

The Harskeel grinned. Finally!

Deek suddenly became agitated, and Wikkell had no notion of what the cause might be. The giant worm thrashed about in the boat.

"What is it?" Wikkell asked. "Do you want to say something?"

The worm did what the cyclops had come to recognize as a nod.

"Very well. I shall put ashore so that you may find a patch of rock."

Wikkell did just that, and moments later Deek

was able to produce that scratching and hesitant voice of his.

"Th-the f-f-fish!"

"What about it? Just a dead creature."

It was difficult for Deek to speak at great length, given the method he had to use. How best to explain that their quarry could not possibly have had a boat, nor any means of constructing one when they had first arrived at the Sunless Sea? And that some of the gouges on the body of the dead fish were, in retrospect, hardly likely to have been made by others of its kind? Best get right to the point: "Th-their b-b-boat!"

Wikkell, for all his size, was not in the least stupid. Despite Katamay Rey's thoughts to the contrary, one did not rise to become first assistant to a wizard by being less than adept. He understood Deek's reference immediately.

"You think so?"

The more Deek thought about it, the more certain he was. "Y-y-yes."

Wikkell digested this unpleasant tidbit, then nodded. "Aye, it would make a certain kind of sense. We should at least check out the possibility, should we not?"

"I-i-indeed."

Wikkell altered his stroke with the oar and the light craft turned quickly. In a moment they were heading back the way they had come. Clever humans, if they could use a dead fish for a raft. Mayhap more clever and therefore more dangerous than they had been given credit for. It might be wise to take extreme care when at last they were approached. It would be foolish to worry about Rey's anger only to be skewered by some sword-wielding human.

On the Sunless Sea, the wizard Katamay Rey was carried over a never-ending dock, accompanied by his thralls the cyclopes. Ahead, the bridge appeared . . . behind, it vanished . . . and it was as if they moved across the most solid of ground.

Chuntha's raft of living worms churned through the water, driven by the magicked screw, keeping far enough behind the wizard to avoid being seen but close enough so that he was but a few moments ahead at any given time.

"There," Red said, flapping a membranous wing toward three openings on the face of the cliff set back slightly from the edge of the water. "The center hole."

"You are certain?" the Harskeel asked.

"Without a doubt."

"Good. Then let us proceed apace."

"Uh, I feel that our bargain has been completed," Red said. "We provided transportation upon the water, and now that journey is at an end."

"But we have not yet captured our prey."

"Your prey," Red observed.

The Harskeel considered its options. Did it need the bats any further? Well, who could tell? Better to have them and not need them than to be without and require their assistance. "I feel that my concentration is too poor to perform the blood-spell transfer at the moment."

Red looked dubious, as dubious as it is possible

for a monkey-sized bat to look. "Oh? And what would aid your concentration? No, allow me to guess: capture of the three tasties?"

"How astute you are."

Red nodded. "I see."

"Barrels of blood in infinite supply," the Harskeel said. "It would be a shame to perhaps mislearn the spell and ruin it, would it not?"

This statement took Red a bit longer to think about. "Very well. We shall accompany you."

"A bat after my own heart."

"Not a bad idea at all."

"Pardon?"

"Nothing. Let us hurry and catch them."

"What in the world is *that*?" Elashi asked, pointing.

Just ahead of them the narrow cave widened into a large chamber. Centered in the room were several tall and spiky-looking, thick-stalked plants. Glow-fungus grew thick upon the walls here, and the plants were easy to see. Upon the floor, surrounding the plants, lay what appeared to be a shimmery carpet that covered the rocks with a soft blanket. Conan had seen that material somewhere before, and it only took an instant for the youthful Cimmerian to recall where: the boat in which the cyclops and worm had ridden seemed most similar.

"Uh-oh," Tull said.

"I do not like the sound of that," Conan said. "What is the problem?"

"These be Webspinners," Tull said.

"So?" Elashi said.

"I know little about them save that they are best avoided, can the Whites and the bats be believed."

At that moment Conan heard someone call him. *Conan.*

He looked around. There was no one here save the three of them.

Conan of Cimmeria. Strong, handsome, manly Conan.

The voice was female, laden with honey and desire, and Conan felt a great puzzlement. Where was the woman who called? He would very much like to know, since it seemed as if she would be well worth getting to know better. A lot better.

Here, Conan. Behind the beautiful plants just ahead of you. Come to me and I shall fulfill your every desire. Pleasure beyond any you have ever known.

Conan blinked. So brazen! He had never known even a trull who so blatantly offered herself to him.

The big Cimmerian glanced at Elashi. No doubt she would not find this woman's call so appealing, and Conan expected to hear of her displeasure quickly and in full measure. But no, Elashi seemed to be caught up in her own thoughts, staring off at the plants as if she could not hear the woman calling to them. Even as he watched, Elashi took a step toward the Webspinners.

Then, next to him, Tull also started forward.

Abruptly, Conan felt a sense of wrongness about that voice.

Fear not, mighty warrior, came the soft tones. *Do not concern yourself with these two. They will not come between us. It is you I want, and you whom I shall serve in any manner you desire.*

Elashi and Tull walked toward the pale carpet, ignoring each other.

"Hold a moment," Conan called to his friends.

Neither slowed, and Conan knew that the shadow of danger lay upon them. That voice—he had not heard it with his ears, but within his head! It was a trap of some kind.

Conan drew his blued-iron sword and leaped forward.

"Tull! Elashi! Stop!"

The Harskeel and its men and bats moved through the narrow corridor. They were of necessity strung out some distance since the bats could not fly were they bunched too close together. If Red's information held true, they would shortly come upon Conan and his friends.

It was all the Harskeel could do to keep from laughing. It urged its men to greater speed.

"There," Wikkell said, pointing to the shore.

The dead fish bobbed slightly as it slowly spun along the edge of the waterway. Now that he looked closer, Wikkell could see the indentations that must have been carved by something other than the teeth of a predator.

The cyclops rowed the boat ashore. He and Deek exited the craft. "There is almost no current in the water. They must be around here somewhere."

"B-b-back th-the w-w-way w-we c-c-came?" Deek suggested.

"That makes sense. We did not pass them beyond.

Let us return to the water. We can move much faster that way."

"A-a-agreed."

Conan's protective reaction was somewhat short-sighted. He leaped past his friends and turned to face them. "Hold!" he ordered, his voice echoing in the quiet cave. But . . . what if they did not? What was he to do, cut them down?

Fortunately, both Elashi and Tull seemed stunned by the force of Conan's shout. They stopped moving just as they reached the floor covering and shook their heads, as if awakening from a dream.

Conan, pay these two no mind! I am waiting for you.

The heretofore velvet-toned voice seemed somewhat terse and irritated in Conan's mind.

"Move back," Conan said. He looked down and noted that he now stood on the strange overlay upon the stone floor.

Elashi screamed. "Conan! Behind you!"

The big Cimmerian spun, sword raised, in time to see a pale and thick green-tinted rope hurtling toward him. The cable flew true, but as it would have draped itself over Conan's shoulder, he swung the sharp iron and hit the thing solidly. The hawser seemed as solid as wood, but the force of Conan's shoulders and arms drove the razor-edged sword; the rope sheared cleanly on impact. The severed section brushed past, touching Conan's wrist and tearing away a patch of skin as it fell. He felt something sticky on his hand where the rope had touched.

Elashi had drawn her own sword, and Tull his

dagger, and all three strove to move away from the danger. Another rope was launched—from a hole in the trunk of the nearest plant, Conan saw— and then a third and a fourth.

"Quick, it's some kind of web!" Conan said, scrambling to attain the bare rock, as did Elashi, but Tull slipped on the smooth coating over the floor and fell. As he did, one of the cast lines landed on him. The rope adhered to Tull's tunic as if a part of it, and the slack in the cable vanished. Tull began to slide toward the plants.

Conan sprang toward the captured man and hewed downward with his blade, catching the rope. It took two cuts to sever it.

In his mind, Conan heard: *Sisters! Aid me! These are the ones worth months' of food.* There was no seduction in that voice, only menace.

Five, six, a dozen more sticky ropes jetted toward the trio. Tull scrabbled to his hands and knees and ran doglike away from the plants. Two of the ropes flew past, missing him and Conan, and the Cimmerian realized that the floor covering was of the same material as the lines and, as well, a measure of the extent of the lines' reach. He darted past Tull, scooped him up with one arm, and leaped for the closest patch of bare rock. One of the ropes tore a leather scrap from his boot, but then they were out of range.

"Gods all!" Elashi said.

The three stared at the plants.

Wait, came that too-sweet voice to Conan again. *This is all a mistake. Come to me and feel the depths of pleasure.*

Conan looked at Elashi. "Do you hear that?"

She nodded. "The powerful voice of a desert chief," she said. "Asking me to be his bride and firstwife."

Conan glanced at Tull. "And what do you hear?"

"A wench who would render me unconscious with her lusts," Tull said.

Conan nodded. He understood it now. The plants emitted some kind of lure to attract victims. Those so attracted would no doubt become sustenance for the plants in short order.

No, came the voice. *You are not to be eaten. Believe us.*

"I think not," Conan said. He turned back to his friends. "Best we go back and find another route."

But as the trio turned to go back the way they had come, a bat chittered and swooped out of the tunnel toward them. After a moment more bats followed, and there came the cries of men.

Conan shook his head and raised his sword. Was there no end to this madness?

Thirteen

It was Deek who spotted the exits from the cavern. Wikkell angled in toward the shore, beached the craft, and he and Deek alighted.

"Th-they m-m-must h-have g-g-gone th-there."

"What makes you so certain?"

"L-l-look."

Wikkell quickly noted what the worm was indicating. The shore, such that it was, virtually disappeared a short distance past the three holes in the rock above them, leaving a sheer cliff face dropping straight into the water. They would have to have the agility of flies to stick to that wall. If their prey had truly come this way, the only method left to them would be to swim a considerable dis-

tance, and Wikkell did not think that likely. They
had not gotten this far by being particularly stupid.

"Aye. But which hole?"

"O-o-one i-is a-as g-g-good a-a-as a-another."

Wikkell nodded. "The one to the right, then?"

"W-w-why n-not?"

The climb was fairly easy for Wikkell, but it
took a bit longer for Deek. When they finally attained the orifice, Wikkell noted that it was rather
dark within.

"I shall go back down and scrape up some
glow-fungus."

"N-n-no n-need. I c-c-can s-s-see w-w-well e-
enough."

"I shall follow your lead, then."

The two of them entered the passage.

Bad luck rode the wings of the first four bats to
swoop at Conan. The first attacker became two
half bats as he was split lengthwise by the Cimmerian's blade. The second and third bats pulled
out of their dives to avoid the deadly sword, but in
so doing, they flew within range of the plants and
their sticky lines; the plants wasted no time in
snaring the hapless bats in their ropes. The fourth
bat managed a tight turn, grinning as he avoided a
line cast by the Webspinners. The grin disappeared
as Conan slashed again, removing the bat's head
from its shoulders. The hurtling body sailed into
the first pikeman to arrive, knocking him flat.

Elashi and Tull cut with their own weapons.
Conan had time to see Tull open the belly of a bat
and Elashi's steel take the wing and leg of another.

The racket smote Conan's ears: screaming bats,

yelling men, the hiss of plant ropes thrown through the dank air. Even so, he grinned. This was something he could deal with, a direct threat, and it was far better to meet an enemy face-on than to continue skulking about in these blasted caves forever.

With that, Conan stepped forward and whipped his blade back and forth at the next wave of bats.

One of the pikemen charged toward Tull and Elashi, pike extended to impale them. Conan smiled as he saw his two friends leap aside, except that Tull stuck his foot out and tripped the attacker. The unfortunate man stumbled and managed to keep his footing but only after he had run a good dozen overbalanced paces onto the silken floor covering. A pair of sticky ropes flew and connected with the pikeman. Plant food he was, and nobody's fault save his own.

No time to think about that. Back to the business at hand!

The Harskeel was altogether enraged: two of its men were down; the other two hopped around like dancers, failing to engage the barbarian and his friends; and the bats were dropping like cut wheat. The Harskeel had drawn its own blade, but it felt no confidence in its men or the bumbling bats. Time for magic, it decided, and quickly!

In the Harskeel's belt pouch were two glass vials: one was of shroud powder, the other of sundust. Tossed against a hard surface, the former would explode into pitch blackness, the latter into brilliant light. Were the Harskeel to use the sundust here in the cave, that brightness would certainly blind any who gazed upon it. Conan and the other two would be easier to deal with were they sightless.

The Harskeel pulled the vial from its belt and raised it for the throw. They must be looking in its direction for the magic to work, so attention must be paid.

"Conan!" the Harskeel screamed.

Hearing his name, the barbarian glanced away from the bat he had just cut down. The sound of its voice calling Conan also drew looks from the man and woman next to him. Good!

The Harskeel threw the vial.

On the Sunless Sea, Katamay Rey felt a disturbance in the air. It was a distance ahead, but he was certain that it concerned his quest. To his bearers he said, "Faster! Your best speed!"

The two cyclopes who carried him complied. Because the dock created never-ending extensions of itself at whatever the speed of its occupants, the party began to move at a run, a pace considerably faster than any man could manage.

Chuntha stopped her living raft at a turning in the waterway and stepped ashore. She moved to the cover of a boulder half eaten away by water dripping from the far ceiling, and peeped around the rock to see how far ahead Rey's party had moved. She expected to see him no more than a short distance away, but she was surprised. The wizard had gained considerably; more, he and his one-eyed trolls now moved at more than twice the speed he had been traveling at earlier. Sensha curse him! What was he up to now?

The witch ran back to her raft and increased the turning of the screw that powered her craft. Whatever he had in mind, she would not be left behind!

The raft of worms churned out into the waterway and moved rapidly around the turning.

"M-m-may all th-the g-gods D-d-damn!"

"What is it?"

The giant worm halted his slither and spoke to Wikkell. "I-it's a-a d-d-dead e-end," he said. "Th-the p-p-passage n-n-narrows j-just a-a-ahead."

"Is there no alternate passage?"

"N-n-none."

"Well, Misha curse it. We will have to go back and try the next passage."

"L-l-let u-us h-h-hurry."

Indeed, Wikkell thought, let us do precisely that.

The vial that the Harskeel tossed flew through the air to smash against the rock exactly where it had aimed. The Harskeel closed its eyes and further covered them with an arm in anticipation of the blinding flash. One, two, three, that should do it!

But when the Harskeel jerked its arm down and opened its eyes, what greeted it was blackness as thick as cold tar.

Curse all the gods! It had thrown the wrong damned vial!

The cave suddenly went black, and Conan spun about in wonder. That creature, the Harskeel, had tossed something at the floor that must be the cause of the instant night. But ... why? It was magic, right enough, and potent, but how could darkness favor the Harskeel?

Conan did not want to wait around to find out. He whispered. "Elashi! Tull!"

"Here," Elashi whispered back.

"And here," Tull said.

"Move toward me. I think I can lead us past them."

There was considerable thrashing about in the darkness as various beings tried to move without hitting a wall or each other. The bats had a certain expertise, but even they must have relied somewhat upon their eyes. Conan heard thumps as bats hit things in the curtain of night that had enveloped them.

"Conan?"

"Here, Elashi."

The woman was very near, and Conan reached out and found her. His hand touched her breast.

"Not now, goat."

"Good that you can joke at a time like this," he said.

At that point Tull blundered into Elashi's backside; Conan could feel the impact as the desert woman was pushed against him.

"Hey!"

"Sorry, lass."

"Hold hands," Conan commanded. "Elashi, grab my hand."

They linked themselves together, and Conan began to edge away from the Webspinners. His sense of direction guided him, that innate knowledge he had, and even though he bumped into things in the darkness—rocks, dead bats, a semiconscious pikeman—he led his party into the tunnel and away from the chaos.

Behind them, Conan heard the Harskeel screaming for its men and the bats to block the passage, but it was already too late.

Deek and Wikkell neared the entrace to the cul-de-sac they had taken. Before they reached their intended exit, however, Wikkell pulled the worm to a halt. "Wait," he said. "I hear something."

Carefully the two of them inched closer to the opening. At this stage of their quest, a strange noise might well be worth much trouble, and they agreed without speaking to exercise extreme caution. Wise that the cyclops and worm did so; the phrase "much trouble" was more than a bit euphemistic, considering what awaited them.

On the edge of the rocky shoreline was a wooden dock, doubtless magically created for it had not been there before. Upon the dock stood Katamay Rey, surrounded by several of Wikkell's brothers; more of the cyclopes stood upon rocky ledges.

Wikkell uttered a whispered epithet, the common and impolite word for excrement, and backed hastily into a deep shadow. Deek agreed with the curse and slid back as quickly as did Wikkell.

"We are doomed," Wikkell whispered.

Deek's scraping on the rock was muted, but it seemed abnormally loud to Wikkell. "P-p-perhaps n-not. L-l-look."

It took the cyclops a moment to understand. The focus of the folk gathered below did not seem to be

upon the tunnel entrance in which Wikkell and
Deek were huddled. No, the assemblage below appeared to be focused upon the center orifice. Wikkell
and Deek's feeling of relief was tempered by the
knowledge that this was both good and bad. Good
because perhaps Rey did not know they were here;
bad because it must mean he did know that the
humans everyone had been chasing around the caves
for what seemed like forever must be in the next
tunnel over. That Rey had to come and fetch them
himself boded ill for Wikkell; that Rey might capture the men offered Deek no hope for pleasing
Chuntha. A bad scenario whichever way it was
constructed.

The thoughts of worm and cyclops were interrupted then as several of the cyclopes gave voice
to rumbles, acknowledging the arrival of newcom-
ers upon the scene. Neither Deek nor Wikkell could
see who these folk might be, but they could certainly guess. It appeared that the game was over.

"I think, Deek my friend, that we are in trouble."

"Y-y-you h-have s-s-said it, f-f-friend."

Katamay Rey smiled at the surprise on the faces
of the three who appeared in the mouth of the
tunnel. They had apparently not been expecting a
reception, two men and a woman, but their shock
did not last. The larger of the men drew a dark-
bladed sword, while the woman and the second
man also produced weapons nearly as fast. Doubtless they could cause some damage to his minions
with those, Rey thought, and the cyclopes, in their
enthusiasm to capture the trio, might also injure
one or more of them. After all the efforts expended

upon this quest, the wizard had no intention of seeing his prey damaged until he had a chance to attend to that personally. He saw the big man gather himself as if to leap down upon the first of the approaching cyclopes. No, that would not do, not at all.

Katamay Rey waved his hands and uttered several words in a language whose last native speaker had died a thousand years earlier. A net flickered out of the air, a coarse-meshed affair stronger than tempered steel and impervious to edged weapons. The net fell upon the three people above, entangling them as they tried to move.

Like much of his magic, the use of this spell exhausted certain supernatural elements of the air in the vicinity. Beneath Rey's feet, the dock quivered slightly but held firm after a moment. Too much magic in any given place depleted that area's store of etheric energies for a time, as a wine bottle is emptied of liquid. One had to be careful lest one create a spell that rendered further magic impossible for a time. Best to always have a reserve for emergencies. Well, no matter. He had the three now, finally. . . .

"Bring them down," Rey ordered. Half a dozen of the cyclopes hurried to comply.

The three within the net struggled to escape, but it was a wasted effort. Until he dissolved the magical device, they were not going anywhere.

Katamay Rey smiled. Whatever threat these three had posed to his control of the Black Caves was certainly past.

*   *   *

Chuntha observed Rey's capture of the three she sought with more than a small amount of irritation. Sensha blast him! He had beaten her to the quarry!

The naked witch slid behind a convenient boulder and considered her options. Because he was first did not mean he was the winner; the issue would not be resolved until he achieved his own stronghold, with its magical wards. Until then, Rey was dangerous but not unbeatable. She had surprise with her; at the proper moment an attack could be mounted against the wizard that would disrupt whatever plans he had.

Timing was, of course, critical; a mistake could be costly. Still, Chuntha did not despair. She had a few tricks of her own packed away, and the thought of destroying That Bastard once and for all caused a warm glow in her belly. She would have her quarry—two men and a woman, each useful—and with proper planning, Rey would have an unplanned and permanent trip straight to Gehanna.

A most pleasant thought.

Fourteen

The Harskeel's anger filled it to capacity. When the shroud powder's effect faded, it found itself looking upon a scene of carnage. None of its men remained alive. Of the four, one had been cut down by the barbarian, the plants had apparently taken another, the bats in their confusion had fastened to a third, and the fourth lay trampled upon the rocky floor. More than a few bats lay dead as well. Red was not one of them.

The bat with whom the Harskeel had bargained hopped toward the man, surveying the dead as he came. "Bad business," Red said.

The Harskeel could not trust itself to speak.

"Well, what say we just take our spell and call it quits, eh?"

e Harskeel's voice came out, but it came
l precisely, the antithesis of its enraged
 feelings. "I have another spell. This one is somewhat different in effect. It turns bats into insects."

"You jest."

"Would you perhaps like a demonstration? Upon
yourself, for instance?"

Red spent little time considering this. "Uh, no. I
shall take your word for it."

"Good. Then let us go and capture this barbarian before I decide that all of the bats in this
blasted cave would serve me better as butterflies!"

Wikkell and Deek watched as the three captives
were carried to the magical dock. Their weapons
were removed and the net dissolved by the wizard,
but only after each human was safely in the grip of
a pair of cyclopes. Even the largest one's struggles
availed it little against the strength of Wikkell's
brothers, and the man seemed to realize this, and
was still.

As the worm and the cyclops watched, Rey and
the group walked to the end of the dock, which
was magically lengthened, the rear section vanish-
ing like so much smoke in a vent breeze. In a few
moments the procession was nearly out of sight.

"N-n-now wh-what?"

Wikkell sighed. "We are in deep trouble, I would
say. You cannot go home, for your mistress will
doubtless be unhappy with you."

"Th-that p-p-puts it m-mildly."

"Nor can I return to my own caves, since the
wizard himself had to come and fetch those I was
sent after. He has no use for failure."

"Wh-what a-are w-we to d-do, th-then? Live as o-o-outcasts?"

"Well, better outcasts than not at all, but I confess that scrounging a living on our own has little appeal for me."

"I-I a-agree."

Wikkell nodded, and the idea that had been nebulously floating about in his head took on more solidity. "Ever wonder how much better off we would all be had not the witch and the wizard ever come to reside here in the caves?"

"M-m-more th-than o-once."

"Or, since that is wishful thinking, were they to leave, or perhaps destroy each other?"

"M-more w-w-wishful th-th-thinking."

"Perhaps not. Neither of us can go home again while those cursed two inhabit the caves. Our lives are practically worthless. As such, might not we try and spend them in a manner that might benefit both our peoples?"

"A-a-are y-you s-suggesting r-r-revolution?"

"I am indeed. What have we to lose?"

Deek considered this. Wikkell's idea, which would have seemed hopelessly absurd only a few days past, did not now sound quite so insane. Not when the only other choice was to spend the remainder of one's allotted time slithering from shadow to shadow against the day when either Chuntha or Katamay Rey would discover and thus put a quick end to them.

"Not to put too fine an edge on it, Deek, but . . . it is either them or us, and given my current thoughts on the matter, I would rather it be them."

"I-I a-agree," Deek said. And why not?

...en, let us see what we can do to gather

Every so often Conan tensed his muscles and tried to break free of the two cyclopes holding him, but he might as well be trying to fly by flapping his arms for all the good it did. They had a grip like iron, and he was in no position to kick them where it would hurt the most.

Elashi and Tull fared no better, and Conan's smiles did not seem to particularly reassure them. The future did not shine brightly at the moment. Then again, the Cimmerian had been in difficulties at least this bad before and had survived to live another day. Who could say? There was little point in worry since it would not help, and he would better spend his energies preparing to seize any opportunity to better their situation. Even free and with his blade, defeating these giant one-eyed beings, not to mention the wizard, might not be the easiest thing he had ever done, but one had to assume that anything was possible.

Chuntha watched from concealment as the wizard and his troop went past. The time was not yet ripe, but it would happen before Rey reached the safety of his own caves. She would make it happen.

The Harskeel and its entourage of Bloodbats reached the mouth of the tunnel that led to the Sunless Sea in time to observe Katamay Rey and his prisoners departing the scene. Red identified the wizard and indicated that irritating the same would be paid with dire consequences.

The Harskeel thought it would explode from the anger within it. Fortunately, it managed to keep its temper. Why did the gods thwart it so? Was that a part of the curse, somehow kept secret from it?

"Very well, we shall follow them and seek an opportunity."

"An opportunity to do *what*?" Red asked.

"Never mind. Just get the boat into the water."

As the Harskeel and the bats entered the water and started after the wizard, Deek and Wikkell watched from within their small cave.

"I wonder how this strange-looking man figures into all this. Doubtless you recall him or her or it, whatever it is, from the encounter in the bat cave?"

"I-I-I r-recall. A-a p-p-puzzle."

For his part, Katamay Rey was feeling very pleased with himself. He had captured the three with more ease than he had anticipated, given Wikkell's failure to do so. He looked forward to inspecting and questioning them at his leisure once in his own chambers, and doubtless that would provide him with many hours of amusement. The big one, especially, should last quite a while before he gave up the spirit.

Then the ceiling of the cave just ahead rumbled and dropped several large rocks into the water, splashing the dock-walkers. Almost immediately, a screaming apparition fell from the hole opened high above, coming right at them!

Rey's surprise was such that even the most basic defensive spells escaped him. He barely had time

warding-off motion with his hands. It
.ent to change the path of the shrieking
.. slightly, so that it missed the dock and hit
ιne adjacent water. Still, the attack was enough to
startle all those who beheld it. These included the
cyclopes attending to the prisoners.

Rey's attention to the attack from above slowed
his gaze at the prisoners for a single beat too long.

Conan's guards had relaxed their hold enough
for him to free one arm. The second guard had a
firmer grip, but unfortunately for him, Conan was
able to twist about and bring his booted foot into
contact with the most sensitive part of males of
virtually all upright species. The cyclops, for all his
size and power, gave voice to an almost girlish
screech at the strike and suddenly found better
uses for his hands than holding on to Conan. The
cyclops clutched at himself, doubled over, and
moaned.

Conan was already moving. He leaped at the
single cyclops holding Elashi and repeated the strike
that had worked so well before. This cyclops was
faster, but in order to protect his ability to sire
children, he let go of Elashi to block Conan's foot.
That was all the Cimmerian needed, and at the
last moment he pulled the kick and threw his
weight instead into a shove. Big as the cyclops
was, he was too close to the edge of the dock to
withstand Conan's full weight. The hapless cyclops
teetered on the edge of the dock and then fell into
the water.

Elashi, meanwhile, went for the weapons. In the
confusion following the attack from above, the des-

ert woman managed to collect the swords and Tull's knife. She tossed Conan his blade, and the brawny Cimmerian began whipping it back and forth at the cyclopes holding Tull. Said guards wanted no part of Conan's sword, and they hastily released their charge.

"Into the water!" Conan yelled.

Tull and Elashi obeyed, the latter despite her inability to swim.

Despite the noise and surprise, they stood little chance of escaping since the wizard was beginning to recover his wits, and there was, after all, no place for the three to go. Conan surfaced, towing Elashi with his sword held over her chest, and paddled furiously for the nearest shore. He expected a bolt of magical energy to sear him into ash at any moment, but he kept moving.

Chuntha saw her chance. Something had dropped from above, coming down almost on top of the wizard, and while he and his troops milled about in confusion, the gorgeous man and the other two managed to free themselves and leap into the water. Good! She could give Rey something else to keep his attention while the three attained the shore; she could then collect them later.

The witch increased the speed of her worm raft and churned toward the magical dock just ahead. She removed from her bags a cork-and-wax-stoppered ceramic jar containing a fog spell. She smiled as she saw the wizard catch sight of her.

"It's the witch! I knew this was her doing!"

The wizard raised his hands to cast a spell, but Chuntha beat him to it. She jerked the stopper from the jar and the fog boiled out explosively. She quickly recorked the jar, but in an instant the area around both worm raft and dock was enshrouded in thick, wet grayness, effectively rendering both wizard and witch invisible to each other.

"Set curse you, bitch!"

"And you, you bastard!"

A magical lightning flashed as Rey tried to wipe away the fog, but Chuntha countered with another blast of fog from the jar. Between those actions and the forces needed to maintain the dock and her boat, the available magic in the immediate area dropped rapidly. Nobody was going to be doing any heavy spellwork for a while, not here.

Time to depart, Chuntha, she told herself. Go and find that big, fine-looking man. . . .

Scurrying along the shore of the waterway, the Harskeel saw the fog in the distance. Now what? it wondered. Where was that cursed bat when it needed him? It quickened its pace.

Conan swam to a shallow ledge upon which he could stand, Elashi in tow. He set the woman upon her feet. Tull arrived a moment later. "What happened?" he asked.

"I know not," Conan replied, "nor do I care. Let us find a path away from here."

"Aye," Elashi said.

From the fog-shrouded water just behind them came a voice: "A good idea from a man who probably has less brain than a turnip."

Conan spun about, his sword pointing into the fog. That voice . . . he knew it from somewhere . . .

Elashi recognized it first. "Lalo!"

Indeed. As he watched, Conan saw the cursed man they had met at the inn only a few days past emerge from the fog and wade toward them. Had it only been a few days? It seemed half a lifetime.

"What are you doing here?" Elashi asked.

"I thought I would drop in and surprise you," Lalo said, "although I am certain almost everything surprises your apelike companion there. What is going on here?" He grinned his perpetual grin, and even Conan had to return a smile.

"I shall explain and introduce you to Tull later," Conan said. "At the moment I think it best we leave before the fog clears."

"Come, come, Conan, does the fog ever clear for you?"

Elashi laughed, and that surprised Conan not in the least. These two should marry. She would be more than a match for the straw-haired fellow.

Deek and Wikkell proceeded in their silken boat, but more cautiously than before, sculling slowly. They arrived in the vicinity of the confrontation between their respective mistress and master, nay— make that ex-mistress and ex-master—as the final wisps of magical fog began to clear from the water. They were in time to see Chuntha leaving rapidly upon a raft made of what looked like two dozen of Deek's brothers and Rey directing his moving dock toward the nearest shoreline.

"I wonder what happened here."

Deek could not speak in the boat, but his curiosity was no less than Wikkell's. He waved his tail in agitation.

"I agree," Wikkell said. "Best we not get too close. They don't see us, and I for one would prefer to keep it that way. Let us find a cove or small bay and lay low."

Wikkell turned the small boat. He glanced over his shoulder. "Not that it matters any longer," he said, "but I do not see the people we were sent to fetch. I wonder if they have escaped? We might still find them."

Deek shook his head in negation.

"You're right. We are committed now. Although perhaps we might induce those three to help us. They seem very lucky, and it would not hurt to have them on our side."

If we happen to run into them, Deek thought.

"If we happen to run into them," Wikkell said.

Odd, Deek thought. They were beginning to think a lot alike. This might well be the start of a beautiful friendship—assuming they lived long enough to enjoy it.

Fifteen

Cull's immediate reaction upon attaining dry land was to flee back toward the place where they had been captured. Conan was of a different mind.

"The wizard will expect that," he said. "Better we should proceed in the opposite direction."

Lalo agreed. "Despite your appearance to the contrary, that is actually very clever."

Conan shook his head. Lalo's curse could turn even a compliment into an insult.

The four of them moved quickly along the fogged shore, hoping to be well away before the cover evaporated.

Not five minutes later, another series of tunnels

branched off to their right. Tull turned to Conan. "What do you think?" he asked.

"You're asking him?" Lalo said to Tull. "There must be more than a bit of slack in your wits, old man."

Tull reached for his knife.

"Wait," Elashi said, catching Tull's arm. "Lalo here is under a geas."

"He'll be under the ground if he does not curb his tongue," Tull said.

"He cannot help insulting you—that is his curse."

Tull considered this. "Really? What a strange thing to inflict upon someone."

"Not to interrupt this discussion," Conan said, "but we are apt to suffer much worse if we stand around and allow ourselves to be retaken by the wizard."

"Aye," Tull said. "So which way?"

"That one," Conan said, pointing at the nearest tunnel. He glanced at Elashi to see if she planned to gainsay that, but for once the woman was silent. She was watching Lalo.

Into the tunnel they fled. After twenty minutes the corridor bifurcated, and they chose the right-hand fork and continued on. Shortly the narrow pipe blossomed out into a wide, low-roofed chamber, the floor of which was littered with large, pillow-shaped stones. The four sat upon one of these stones to catch their breath.

"Perhaps one of you nit brains would be so good as to explain what is going on here," Lalo said.

Elashi looked at Conan. "I think he means you," she said.

"You are so much better with words," Conan told her. "You tell him."

"Very well." Elashi explained their adventures of the last few days. Tull added background material about the caves and the ongoing battle between the witch and the wizard. When they were done, Elashi asked Lalo how he had come to be there.

"As it happened, I wore thin my welcome at the village inn. I insulted the owner's ugly daughter once too often and he showed me the door. An old story. So I decided to take the dangerous route, feeling I had not much to lose. I saw evidence of your passage—the dead watchbeast and the Harskeel's men, looking somewhat worse for the local scavengers having been at them. And I passed almost entirely through the area without incident . . . until the ground opened beneath my feet and I fell into the huge lake below. I thought certain my time had come to leave this world for the next. Imagine my surprise when I saw the three of you standing on a dock practically right in my path."

"I can imagine," Conan said. His voice was dry.

"Well, anyway, what has that tiny mind of yours come up with for a way out of here?"

Curse or no curse, if Lalo kept talking that way, Conan doubted if he could maintain his temper much longer. He smiled benignly, though, and said, "At first we merely thought to find a way out, to escape."

"At first?" Elashi and Tull echoed in unison.

"Aye. After that last episode, our plans changed somewhat."

"They did?" Tull and Elashi said.

Conan continued. "Aye, they did. We now have in mind collecting some of the valuables amassed by either the witch or the wizard or both, to pay for our troubles here. *Then* we will leave."

"Are you mad?" Elashi asked.

"Not at all. You will recall Tull telling us that both the witch and the wizard have assorted jewels and gold, collected in their caves through centuries of robbing passersby."

"Aye," Elashi said. "So? You cannot expect to simply stroll into the stronghold of a magician and steal such valuables."

"And why not? The witch and wizard are both out here looking for us, are they not? Recall that worm raft we saw. Think about it—where is the last place you would expect them to look?"

"He is mad," Elashi said to Tull.

Lalo laughed. "Perhaps, but there is nothing wrong with his plan, despite the fact that it was hatched by him. When the farmer is in the field, the hens are ripe for the fox."

"You have taken leave of your senses as well," Elashi said.

Lalo nodded. "Doubtless after years of smiling so. As you might suspect, I have little love for wizards, and being compensated by one pleases me greatly. With enough money, one may insult anyone and get away with it. A rich man can buy companions who will withstand much for sufficient payment. Or mayhap even find another mage who can lift the spell. With great wealth comes great respect. I shall be happy to assist you, you barbarian buffoon."

Conan smiled. "Glad to have your help, Lalo."

Elashi and Tull looked at each other.

"Maybe Conan does have something," Tull said.

Elashi said, "Oh, he has something all right— half the wits of a bedbug!"

"I am open to suggestions," Conan said.

Despite herself, Elashi grinned. She shook her head. "All right, I take your point. I have no better idea. At the moment, anyway."

"Then we shall do it," Conan said. "I think I can direct us back to Tull's hideaway. Can you lead us to the wizard or the witch's chambers from there, Tull?"

"Aye."

"Then let us be on our way."

Conan felt good about his plan. He figured that they owed the witch and the wizard much for all the grief those two had caused them. What better blow to strike than one that would provide financial benefit in the process? As Lalo had said, sufficient money would make a soothing balm. A most soothing balm indeed . . .

Though they had grown used to each other's company, Wikkell and Deek decided that it would be best to return to their own people as soon as possible. With the witch and the wizard away from their chambers, the time would never be better for the worm and the cyclops to approach their own kind with their plans to depose the evil humans.

So when Chuntha and Katamay Rey went deeper into the far reaches of the Sunless Sea searching for the three humans, Deek and Wikkell turned their craft homeward.

They sculled the little boat along until both were hungry and tired, then stopped to make a meal upon assorted fungi and to rest themselves.

"It will not be easy, you realize."

"N-n-no. O-our p-p-people w-w-will b-be a-afraid."

Wikkell nodded and munched upon a brownish mushroom with a slimy cap. "And rightly so. Both the wizard and the witch are powerful. Many of us may die. It will take some convincing. I fear my brothers may feel I am merely trying to save my own hide."

"T-t-true e-enough."

"Certainly. But in the long run, it will be better for us without such tyrants as rulers."

"I-in th-the l-long r-r-run, w-we a-are a-all d-d-dead."

"Yes, to be sure. But look at us, for instance. We get along well enough, though I confess I had mis-givings early on."

"A-as d-d-did I."

"But there is no reason your people and mine cannot be friends, save for those two who rule."

"A-a-agreed."

"We must convince our brothers and sisters to take the long view, Deek. Why, we might even create some kind of joint council, your folk and mine, with input from the plants and perhaps even the bats and Whites. Bring prosperity to the caves, instead of the boots of Rey and Chuntha upon our throats."

"Am-am-ambitious i-idea."

"True. But united, we could certainly defeat even such powerful beings as those two."

"O-one w-w-would h-hope."

Wikkell smiled and the green light played upon his thick teeth. "Here, have some of this slimeball."

"Th-thank y-you, f-f-friend."

Deek caught the succulent fungus in the gash that served his kind for a mouth. Normally the worms kept their mouths hidden under a flap of tough epidermis, never revealing the orifice except to the most trusted of friends or a mate. At this point Deek felt that if he could not trust Wikkell the one-eye, he likely could not trust anyone.

"We might well go down in history," the cyclops said, reaching for another slimeball.

"O-or i-into th-the l-l-lime pits," Deek said.

Yes. There was that, too.

Katamay Rey's anger flowed through him, tempered somewhat by fear. The stranger in the caves—Conan, he had heard the female call him—ran loose once again. A bad sign, considering the crystal's prophesy. Of course it was the witch's fault. Somehow she had caused the ceiling to fall in almost upon them, and her construct or thrall, whichever it had been, had very nearly hit its target, save for Rey's quick warding action. The following attack, with its blasted fog and his counter, had depleted the magical flux so that he had been unable to deal the witch the crushing blow she so justly deserved. In fact, had a bit more of the mantalogical energies been drained, the very dock upon which he stood would have dissolved, and that would have been a fine predicament to have faced.

When at last the fog had cleared, both witch and quarry where nowhere to be seen. There was barely enough flux left to construct the never-ending dock to chase them. The going was slow at first, until the wizard and his cyclopes departed from the defluxed region, back into the farther reaches of the Sunless Sea. Oh, she was going to pay, Chuntha was, and twist properly in the doing of it.

Chuntha's raft had very nearly come apart while battling the wizard. The magical glue had softened and the entire construct had shifted and wobbled before she had enough sense to turn her craft and beat a fast retreat from the immediate area close to Rey. Fortunately, she emerged from the space where the magic had been drained before her raft became a collection of worms once again. The glue solidified and Chuntha sparked the magicked screw to higher rotation. The beautiful barbarian had escaped, and no doubt he and his party would be running for all they were worth, away from the wizard. Chuntha merely had to retrace her earlier course along the waterway until she spotted them, or some trace of them.

She had the advantage of the wizard now, and she meant to utilize it fully. She wondered what that apparition had been falling from the ceiling, but did not worry overmuch about it. Probably some spell Rey had cast incorrectly, and it served him right to have it backfire so. That was not her concern; the man she sought was, and she intended to bring all her energies to bear upon his retrieval.

Having abandoned the raft and taken the route along the shore, the Harskeel arrived at the end of the confrontation between witch and wizard. As the magical fog still enshrouded the scene, the Harskeel realized that there was perhaps more than a bit of danger here for itself and its quest. Quickly the Harskeel ordered the bats dispersed, to return later. It found a large, horseshoe-shaped rock to crawl under and conceal itself.

From out of the fog a raft of giant white worms appeared, bearing a beautiful, naked woman. This craft went back the way the Harskeel had just come.

Moments later the fog dissipated and the wizard was revealed, ranting upon a dock in the middle of the waterway.

Of Conan and his companions there was no sign.

After a moment the wizard began walking upon his dock and a new section of it appeared in front of the marching cyclopes. They followed the path of the witch's worm raft.

Interesting, the Harskeel thought. It had been beyond the edges of the fog, and Conan had not come this way. Since the barbarian was not held captive by either witch or wizard, he must then have gone in the opposite direction. Aha! The witch and the wizard moved in the wrong direction; too bad for them, but not for the Harskeel.

As soon as the wizard moved from view, it would summon those stupid Bloodbats and resume its quest. With luck, it might be some time before wizard or witch realized their error; with more luck, perhaps they would destroy each other, although the Harskeel thought it best not to depend greatly upon that.

The wizard and his cyclopes marched along the magical dock and out of sight. Now, where were those moronic bats?

Sixteen

With his uncanny sense of direction fully operative, Conan managed to lead the party of four through twists and turns that eventually ended at the hideaway Tull had constructed.

Oddly enough, the bat cave, which had to be traversed again, was empty of those winged creatures. Not that Conan particularly cared where they had gotten to, as long as that place lay far away.

"My," Lalo said as he observed Tull's hidden alcove, "quite the nest-maker, are you not? Pity you aren't female, you'd make some man a fine wife."

Tull's smile was obviously forced, and he kept toying with the handle of his dagger.

165

Conan could well see how it would be necessary for Lalo to be an adept in some form of combat. Even when you knew about the curse, Lalo tended to grate upon the nerves in a hurry. To break the tension, Conan asked, "Which is the closer—the witch's abode or that of the wizard?"

"Each is about the same distance from here, I reckon," Tull said.

"Hmm. Then which would likely hold the most booty?"

Tull scratched at his bearded chin, considering the question. "Depends on what you're looking for. The wizard, he has a fondness for gold. It don't tarnish like silver nor rust like iron, and the caves are some damp, as you no doubt have noticed."

"Ah, that sounds promising," Lalo said.

Both Conan and Tull held their silence for a moment, waiting for Lalo to add an insult, but none was forthcoming. That was almost irritating in itself.

"Then again," Tull finally continued, "the witch, she has a liking for precious stones. Rubies, emeralds, fire-rocks, like that."

Conan considered that. Such a choice was most interesting. Gold? Or gems? A dilemma. "Can we perhaps raid both chambers?"

"Madness," Elashi said to Lalo. "Whatever wits he may ever have possessed, they are gone now. Greed makes you stupid, Conan."

Conan ignored her, but Tull's next comment scotched the idea of a dual robbery.

"Not likely," Tull said. "They are maybe the same distance from here, but in different directions. It's two days' march between 'em, easy."

"Too bad," Conan said. "Well, the witch's chambers, then."

Elashi raised one eyebrow at Conan. "Why so?"

It lay upon the top of Conan's tongue to answer that he thought dealing with a witch—a woman—would be easier than dealing with a wizard—a man—should anything go wrong. Recalling his travels with Elashi so far, however, he realized that to speak such reasoning aloud would only irritate her and bring forth an undammed flow of invective. For some reason, Elashi seemed convinced that women were the equal of men in practically all things, and Conan had no desire to listen to another of her tirades. Perhaps, he thought, he was learning to deal with women after all.

"Well?" she said.

Conan thought quickly. "Well-cut jewels are more valuable than gold, and much lighter. We can carry more gems than coin."

That made sense, and Elashi nodded.

Conan kept his face an expressionless mask, though he was smiling inside. There was nothing wrong with the way his mind functioned, Lalo and Elashi's carping to the contrary.

"Then let us wait no longer," Conan said. "Lead on, Tull."

Wikkell's labors among his fellow cyclopes had not been spectacularly successful. Their resistance had been somewhat more than he had anticipated. As he trudged along a back tunnelway to meet Deek, he recalled one of many similar conversations:

"Attack the wizard? *And* the witch? Are you daft?"

"Certainly there is some risk," Wikkell began.

"*Some* risk? By all the demons in Gehanna, Wikkell, those two will certainly turn us into ooze if we dare oppose their will."

"They are but two, and we are many."

"So said the slug about the pair of falling boulders, brother. There is much room upon the floors of these caves for puddles that once were such as we."

It pained Wikkell to hear this, the more so because the speaker was in fact his true brother, born of the same mother only a year after Wikkell himself had been born.

"We shall have aid from the worms."

"Ah, well, that is different, then. You have been eating the black-spoored mushrooms again, haven't you? I trust the worms almost as far as I do the wizard."

In the end Wikkell realized that he was wasting his breath. If he could not convince his own brother of the rightness of his cause, what chance did he have of enrolling others in his plan? And perhaps "plan" was too strong a term. "Vague leaning" might be more appropriate at this stage of the revolution.

He needed some kind of demonstration, something to show the cyclopes that the wizard and the witch were not invulnerable. Could he but demonstrate the smallest crack in their magical armor, it would be enough. No one liked being ruled by the magical iron hand, and if they truly thought a real chance existed to overthrow the tyrant, Wikkell was certain he could convince them.

Well, perhaps Deek had fared better. It would be galling to admit that the worms were more reasonable than his own kind, but he had to admit that such a thing might be possible. He could swallow his pride, he supposed, if Deek could generate more fire among his fellows. It was the end that mattered, after all.

Not long now, Wikkell thought. The prearranged meeting place lay only a few minutes ahead. It was an out-of-the-way spot, unlikely that anyone would accidentally happen upon them, which is why they had chosen it.

Wikkell sighed and tried to think of the best way to break his bad news to the worm.

In the small grotto, hidden from prying eyes, Deek arrived to find Wikkell already waiting. Too bad. Ah, well, there was no help for it. He had to tell his one-eyed friend the bad news.

They exchanged greetings, and Deek settled himself upon a particularly resonate patch of rock.

"M-m-my b-b-brothers th-th-think I a-am m-mad."

"Oh, no. I was hoping—" Wikkell stopped.

"H-h-hoping wh-what?"

"That you would have better success than I. My fellows also think me less than sane."

"Th-they w-w-won't h-help?"

"I'm afraid not. And from your comments, I assume the same is true of your folk?"

"S-s-sad, b-but t-t-true."

"Damn them all to Gehanna. Now what are we going to do?"

Deek had pondered that thought long and hard, and his conclusion involved more than a little personal risk. He said, "W-w-we h-h-have t-to sh-show th-them."

Wikkell nodded. "My thoughts as well. Can we but demonstrate that the witch and the wizard are not all-powerful, we have a chance."

"G-g-got a-any i-ideas?"

"Plenty, though I suspect most are apt to get us killed. I should like to avoid such a thing if at all possible."

"I-I-I t-too w-would a-avoid s-s-such an e-ending."

"Well, then, let me put forth my thoughts and then listen to yours. We are resourceful, after all. Surely we can come up with *some*thing."

Deek nodded. Indeed, he thought. High time to either defecate or slide out of the scat trench. No two ways about it.

"Here is my first idea . . ."

The blasted bats took their time returning to where the Harskeel lay in hiding. Travels would have to be on foot or in the air. The Harskeel did not trust itself to the bats' ability to safely carry it, so that meant it would have to walk.

Being enraged seemed to have become the Harskeel's permanent mental state, and it feared that its anger might cause it to do something foolish. The Harskeel made an effort to calm itself. All right. The quarry had escaped once again; at least its two competitors for Conan had been put off the scent. Its men were all dead, true, but there were the bumbling bats to replace them. That might be rather like exchanging a half-wit for an idiot, but one had to make do as best one could. All in all, the Harskeel reflected, things were no worse than ever they had been. No better perhaps, but no worse. When at last it captured its prey, the end would justify all of these rigorous means, certainly.

With those thoughts trying and mostly failing to calm its anger, the Harskeel set off after Conan and his friends.

Urging the worm raft to its utmost speed, Chuntha scanned the banks of the Sunless Sea, searching for signs of her elusive quarry. She knew not how far the waterway extended, never having followed it to its end in all the years she had resided below the ground. She often thought of the sunlit world above, and how happy she had been there, plundering the bodies of willing men for their carnal spirits. Unfortunately, she could not run around naked up there any longer, civilization having curtailed that option, and worse, too many bodies aroused suspicion. More than once she had fled from a city or a village with the local folk chasing her, hot for her death.

The underground had disadvantages, to be sure, but once she managed to wrest total control of it from the wizard, she could arrange to have a steadier supply of bedmates than before. Few men would risk the caves to retrieve a lost traveler, and Chuntha knew she could snag the odd one now and again without arousing much suspicion. After all, dangerous animals lived up there, and brigands, too; one had to expect that they would take their toll . . .

A dark opening appeared on the cave wall to her right, just ahead. Since her quarry now traveled on foot, such an exit might well appeal to them. The problem was that she could not explore every tunnel along the way; there were far too many of them. Fortunately, Chuntha had exactly the thing she needed.

From her supplies she took a tall, black jar and a pair of tweezers. She opened the jar's lid and with the tweezers removed a speck of red the size of a pin's head. She quickly closed the jar and set the red speck upon the deck of her living raft. Uttering a few mystical phrases, Chuntha waved her hands at the speck. In a twinkling it expanded into a red hornet the size of a sparrow. The creature fluttered its wings, buzzing.

"Go," Chuntha commanded. "Explore that tunnel and return to me if you find any human within."

Obediently the giant hornet rose from the raft and jetted away, zipping toward the tunnel in an arrow-straight line. The magicked hornets were of limited value, but useful within those limits. They could be directed for simple tasks such as an in-and-out search of a tunnel. More complex things were beyond their capacity; still, if her beautiful barbarian were in that tunnel, the insect would find him and return to tell the tale.

She had dozens of the creatures within her jar, and she would dispatch as many as it took to locate her quarry. She had obtained the magical beasts after a liaison with a self-styled wizard who had, in bed, sought to match her powers of Sensha. He lost, naturally, and those magics of his she could operate became hers by default. It had been a long time ago, but Chuntha still remembered the man fondly. He had lasted the better part of an hour before dying.

Being that the escapees were on foot, they could not have gone far. They were either in a tunnel close to the place where the wizard had lost them or not far ahead and still fleeing onshore. Either way, Chuntha should be able to find them soon.

She smiled at that thought. She had planned to take the captives back to her chamber, to enjoy them at her leisure, but perhaps not. Perhaps she would take them to the nearest flat spot and have them there.

The thought of it warmed her loins. Yes. Why wait? Better to enjoy them before that stupid wizard perhaps mucked things up again. Afterward her powers would be increased, and she would deal with the hapless Rey.

The worm raft continued along, Chuntha smiling upon its back as she moved over the waters.

Katamay Rey sat in his sedan chair, borne at a fast trot by his cyclopes. He had yet to catch sight of Conan and the others but, he reflected, it should be only a short while before he did so. Of course they could have easily darted into one of the myriad openings along the way. Quite probably they had done so, had they any sense, but that did not worry him. The wizard was not without certain spells to ascertain such things . . .

From his pack of magical impedimenta, Rey withdrew a leather bottle of no small age. He shook the bottle, and a faint buzzing began within. He removed the cork from the narrow-necked vessel and shook it again. A small insect, gnat-sized, emerged from the bottle, which the wizard quickly recorked. Rey spoke a tongue-twisting phrase in a gutteral language and the gnat-sized creature blossomed into a blue wasp the size of a small bird. The giant insect buzzed back and forth, awaiting Rey's command, which was not long in coming.

"Go and explore the first tunnel you find that is large enough to admit a man. Finding any men, return and report it to me immediately."

The blue wasp buzzed and took off, heading toward the shore. Rey smiled at its departure. He had once had another investigatory insect species, a jar of magical red hornets, but he had traded them to a cocks-wizard above ground long ago. The hornets and wasps were antipathetical, and it was possible to use one or the other, but not both simultaneously. The red and the blue insects hated each other and would fight to the death upon meeting. Rey had thought it an unnecessary duplication to have both.

Of course the witch was somewhere in the vicinity, and she would have to be dealt with in the not-too-distant future. He would be better prepared the next time, and she would rue the day she had sought to challenge Katamay Rey!

The cyclopes trotted along the never-ending dock, oblivious to their master's contemplations. For his part, the wizard felt that his quest would be ended shortly. It could not happen soon enough to suit him, either.

Seventeen

Conan's plan was simple, and he saw no need to complicate it. They would travel to the witch's quarters, bypass or dispatch any guards left there, and load their purses and pouches with loot. Having done that, they would depart rapidly and find a place where the roof of some cavern was accessible from below. Here they would dig their way through the roof, which should prove to be the ground above, clamber out, and be gone.

Naturally Elashi had her doubts, and she voiced them quickly, as was her wont. "First, what makes you think we can dispatch any guards so easily? What if this witch has left one or more of those giant worms standing ready to intercept would-be visitors?"

"Recall the giant fish?" Conan said. "If my blade could slay him, it can slay a much smaller legless grub."

"All right, assuming this is so, then there is the matter of our escape. Do you think it so easy to simply dig through the roof and depart these caves? Tull here has been underground for five years. Think you not that he has tried such a maneuver before?"

Conan looked at Tull. "Have you, then?"

"Sort of," Tull answered. "The places where the roof is reachable are few, and while I tried digging in a couple, I could never finish before either a worm or a cyclops came along. Spotting holes, they usually patch 'em, save the ones they make themselves for trapping travelers. Those are always too high to reach, or guarded."

Conan turned back to Elashi. "There are four of us; we can dig much faster than one. Besides, the odd worm or cyclops happening by will pose less of a threat to four."

"You have all the answers, do you?" Elashi was angry.

Conan nodded. As a matter of fact, he did. "Aye, leastways the ones we need, save one: how much farther is our objective, Tull?"

"A few hours' walk."

"Then let us save our breath for walking instead of spending it talking," Conan said.

Elashi frowned at this; Lalo's face kept its perpetual smile, and he said nothing.

Through rocky chambers they traveled, passing under great pointed stalagtites that dripped tiny drops of mineralized water, past walls so thickly covered with glowing fungus that the bright green light generated gave them views clearer than the shining of the full moon.

Once the four passed within a few spans of a solitary Webspinner Plant. Conan heard the seductive but faint call of the carnivorous plant: *Mighty warrior! Come to me and be pleasured beyond belief!* But his earlier experiences made him immune to its beckonings, as were Tull and Elashi.

They warned Lalo but need not have bothered. Lalo paused and appeared to listen for a moment, then answered the mindspeech of the plant aloud: "I have seen better leaves on overripe turnips," he said. "If ever there was an uglier bit of flora, doubtless men would be struck blind upon viewing it."

Lalo's insults sparked an angry response from the Webspinner, and its siren's song became one of outrage: *I shall eat your liver, foul one!*

Apparently no one under Lalo's particular curse had passed this way before. Conan suspected that should the plant be so foolish as to snare Lalo, likely it would choke upon him.

Tull's years of experience in the caverns had given him some knowledge of little-used passages, and the four kept to these, avoiding contact with any of the giant worms. Once they spotted one of the creatures passing by in a cross tunnel, but it did not appear to notice them, intent as it seemed on some destination of its own.

The hours passed, and eventually the four arrived in the vicinity of the witch's personal chambers. Cautiously Conan and Tull crept forward until they could see the entrance to the main chamber.

From behind the cover of a series of large rocks, the pair viewed the scene.

A quad of giant worms lay just outside the entrance.

Conan and Tull slid back and rejoined Elashi and Lalo. These two whispered between themselves, stopping when Conan arrived.

"Well?" Elashi and Lalo said together.

"There are four worms guarding the entrance," Conan said.

"Aha!" Elashi said.

"I foresee no problem," Conan said, somewhat sharply. "The solution is simple. Two of us will draw the worms' attention, allowing the other two to slip inside and plunder the chamber. Tull tells me the worms cannot move so fast as can a running man. After the theft, we shall all rejoin at a prearranged place."

Elashi merely shook her head, while Lalo said, "Conan, you would make the task of marching into Gehanna and slaying the King of the Demons sound like a routine visit to the night chamber."

Elashi found her tongue and managed to get it working. "And who, pray tell, is to lead the worms upon this merry chase? I played fish bait once, and I have no intention of repeating such a performance."

"Tull and I will draw the worms away," Conan said. "I can lead the pair of us to our meeting place later, and surely you and Lalo can manage to pocket a few lightweight stones?"

Lalo chuckled. "I called you a barbarian fool before, but I stand corrected. You are worse, Conan. You are a politician. You should be a king somewhere."

That did not sound much like an insult to Conan, but knowing Lalo, he was certain it must be. He ignored it.

Tull said, "Aye. 'Twould best be done quickly, too. Sooner or later the witch will realize that she has lost our track and turn her attentions this way. Best we be gone 'fore she returns."

Nobody argued with that.

"Let us make ready, then," Conan said.

The Harskeel was no tracker, but it knew that the bats could fly faster than either it or its quarry could move on foot, so it dispatched them forward to search, keeping only Red as a guide.

Red, by this time, chaffed at the Harskeel's commands, and so the Harskeel tried to mollify him.

"I begin to wonder if this blood spell is worth all our efforts," the Bloodbat said.

"You recall the taste. What more can I say?"

"I had not intended to spend the rest of my life on your quest."

"Ah. Well, I can understand that. As a token of my esteem for your assistance, I shall supply you personally with an extra incentive. Naturally I was only joking about turning you into an insect."

"Oh, naturally." The bat's voice held some disbelief.

"I have a small spell you might find amusing. It will make you irresistible to the females of your species."

Red made a noise that the Harskeel took for a laugh. "A waste of your spell," he said, "for I am already irresistible to all females I desire."

The Harskeel suppressed its own laugh. "Ah, of

course. But there is an added effect to the magic: it allows the user to . . . ah . . . maintain a certain . . . potency. Indefinitely."

"Indefinitely, you say?"

"Practically."

Red stared at the Harskeel. "Ah. I see. Well, certainly I have never had any problems in this regard, but I can see where that might be useful."

This time the Harskeel allowed itself to laugh.

Just then one of the other bats returned, jabbering at them in the bat's speech.

"What has it said?"

"Apparently your quarry—your pardon, *our* quarry—stands near the entrance to the witch's chambers."

"What are they doing there?"

"Who knows? We are not mind readers. It is sufficient that they are."

"How much farther is it?"

"Not far. If we hurry, we can be there within the hour."

"Then let us hurry!"

Wikkell and Deek had settled upon a plan that, while risky, carried with it a fair chance of success. They moved along one of the main corridors toward the chambers of the witch, already implementing their idea. Wikkell had wrapped around his wrists—rather loosely, but not obviously so—a length of rope that trailed off into a long leash. The end of this tether lay clamped tightly in Deek's mouth, and from external appearances, it seemed that Deek held Wikkell in thrall.

The plan was simple enough. They would arrive

at the witch's chambers, Wikkell ostensibly a captive. The guard worms knew Deek as a confidant to Chuntha and would normally have little hesitation about admitting him to her sanctum. Deek would indicate that he was supposed to bring his captive to the witch for questioning. Of course, since Chuntha was not inside, he would need to wait for a time.

Once inside the chambers, Deek and Wikkell would steal one of the witch's more prized possessions—some spell or talisman—and then leave, offering the guard worms a story about Chuntha's having summoned them elsewhere. Guard worms were picked for their size and fighting skills, not for their brains, and Deek had little worry that they would impede the plan in either direction.

Then, to finish the plan, they would reverse roles—Wikkell playing captor and Deek captive—and repeat the operation at the chambers of the wizard. It would take another two days at their best speed, but when it was done, each would have a magical talisman from the inner chambers of the ruler opposite. With such devices in hand, convincing their people that they stood a chance against witch and wizard should be much easier. Both Deek and Wikkell had rehearsed their speeches:

"If the wizard/witch is so powerful," they would say, "then how is it that I was able to enter his/her chambers and take this magical implement so easily? He/she is more bluster than bite. We can prevail!"

Admittedly, there was no guarantee that this idea would positively work, but certainly it was a better idea than awaiting the certain end that would befall Wikkell and Deek whenever their respective masters finally got around to wondering about them. A small chance, they thought, was better than none at all.

Several times as they neared the witch's chambers, Deek and Wikkell passed other worms in the main corridor, and each time those other worms readily accepted Deek's fabricated story. It looked as if this plan might work, and as the two kept reminding each other and themselves, they had nothing to lose.

Something, Chuntha realized, was amiss. She had seeded each opening she had passed along the edge of the Sunless Sea with a search hornet. If there was even a suspicion of an exit, she had sent one of her magical insects to check it. So far, each that reported back had failed to detect her prey. Some had not yet returned, but Chuntha began to grow restless. Unless this barbarian could somehow grow wings of his own, it was impossible for him to have traveled this far. Her boat's speed far exceeded that of a walking man, and even a runner would have trouble in maintaining such a pace for long. But . . . if it were not possible for the man and his companions to have passed where she now floated, it could mean only one thing: her quarry had gone the other way.

Chuntha slapped her bare thigh, sending a quiver through the taut muscle. Of course! Why had she not thought of that before? She had assumed that they would flee from pursuit back the way they had come. That assumption could be, she realized now, a mistake.

She wondered if the wizard had also been taken in by the ploy. Had he done so, he would be approaching her even as she sat bestilled thinking of it.

Chuntha sighed deeply. If that were the case, she would have to prepare to battle him now, even without the powerful essence of the barbarian. There was no way to slip past Rey did he come this way, and while she would have preferred to fight him on her own ground, this place was as good as any.

Chuntha bent over her assemblage of magical paraphernalia and began to lay out her most potent items. At least she had surprise on her side. She would find a quiet cove shrouded in shadow and await the wizard's arrival. With luck, she could strike him down before he became aware of her.

Rey reached the conclusion that he moved in the wrong direction before he had dispatched his third wasp seeker. It was not a logical and reasoned decision, but a deeply felt reaction from his gut. He *knew*, by some manner that he could not precisely say, that the one called Conan and the others had gone in the opposite way.

The wizard lost no time in rectifying his error. Immediately he circled on the dock and urged his cyclopian mounts to a run. He was worried. His chambers were guarded, of course, but these newly arrived troublemakers had proved rather resourceful thus far, and the nagging dread brought on by the crystal's prophesy sprang to the fore of his thoughts. What mischief might they do should his guards be overcome? Not a pleasant thought. There were spells in his inventory that could do great damage in untrained hands. In fact, maybe the best solution to this entire affair would be to scurry home as fast as possible and barricade himself into his chambers, backed by the full powers he kept there.

The more he thought about it, the surer he became. If only it was not yet too late!

"Faster!" Rey commanded the cyclopes.

But they were already at their highest speed, and he was jolted back and forth in the sedan by the cadence of their running steps. Of a moment Rey had a dark premonition about all this . . . and he liked it not in the least.

Eighteen

At the turning of the corridor approaching the witch's chambers, Conan and Tull suddenly leaped into view of the four large worms standing guard.

"Yaah!" Conan screamed, whirling his sword overhead.

Tull also hopped about, making meaningless noises and waving his arms.

The worms got the point. The four of them moved as one, scooting across the rocky floor with a speed Conan found rather amazing.

At the first sign of movement, Conan and Tull ran, drawing the worms after them. As they pounded along the rocky floor of the corridor, Conan said, "They move faster than you led me to believe."

185

"Faster than I believed myself," Tull panted.

Indeed, as Conan and Tull rounded another turning of the corridor, the worms cleared the first turning in pursuit. Conan said, "It appears that we won't have to slow to avoid losing them."

Tull glanced over his shoulder as the worms slithered into view behind them. "Mitra! Who would have expected them to be able to slide along so quickly?"

Both men increased their speed and saved their breath for running. They managed to maintain their lead, but just barely, and a slip or slowing now would allow their pursuers to catch them all too quickly.

Elashi and Lalo waited until the guard worms were out of sight, then quickly darted to the entrance of the witch's chambers. Lalo took the lead and in a moment they were inside an antechamber. Glow-fungus covered the walls and the way was easy to discern.

"I hope that the witch did not think to leave magical wards in place," Lalo said, his voice a whisper.

"*Now* you think of this!"

"I did not hear *you* voice such a concern earlier, Elashi dear. Perhaps you have been with Conan too long ... some of his lack of wit may have tainted you."

"I have not the time to properly educate you, you grinning fool," she said. "We have a job to do."

They made their way through the antechamber and into a large and high-ceilinged room. In the center of it lay a large bed of silken cushions, and various items of furniture stood against the walls: chests, dressers, trunks, and an assortment of boxes, large and small.

"This must be the place," Elashi said.

"As always, your perception amazes me. Certainly this is the place."

"Shut up and look for jewels!"

Quickly, the pair of them moved forward.

The Harskeel did not plan to be thwarted this time. Regardless of the cost, it intended to have Conan and his blade. Its idea was not overly complex. When Conan was spotted, the Harskeel intended to launch all of the fifteen or so bats still in its command at the barbarian lout. That Conan would die and be drained of blood quickly was a given, but before he was completely desanguineous, the Harskeel would dart in and seize the barbarian's sword and blood it. A few drops would suffice; it was, after all, not the quantity but the quality of the fluid that mattered. True, the Harskeel would not have the pleasure of watching Conan die slowly, suffering for the grief he had caused, but at this stage of the game, the end was paramount. One sometimes had to forgo the lesser pleasures for the greater. All that the Harskeel desired at this point was to achieve its main goal . . . and then depart these cursed caves forever.

It hurried along the path, eager for the finish to its quest.

Time dragged, and Chuntha began to worry anew. That Bastard should have arrived by now. That the wizard had not marched into her trap bothered the witch greatly. She saw two possibilities: one, that he had somehow been made aware of her and held back, or two, he had also discerned that the quarry he and Chuntha mutually sought had taken another route.

The witch decided that she must know which was the case, and quickly. She plucked one of the red hornets from its prison, enlarged it, and dispatched it with instructions: "Go along this waterway until you see Katamay Rey the wizard. Do not allow him to see you, and return immediately and report."

In an eyeblink the enchanted hornet was gone.

Chuntha sat back down upon the raft and waited.

Rey's thralls made good time. The wizard's trip toward his own chambers progressed rapidly. At one point, over the clop-clop of his cyclopes' heavy tread upon the never-ending dock, he thought he heard a buzzing sound, but when looked around, he saw nothing. It did not matter. That Bitch was still in the area somewhere, but likely far behind him and going in the wrong direction. Surely she had made the same mistake as he, and that was her problem and not his own.

Slowly the guard worms gained upon the two running men. Conan glanced over his shoulder and realized that it would be only a matter of time before the giant beasts overtook him and Tull, an unpleasant thought. They had to do something fairly soon; the older man's labored breathing told the Cimmerian that Tull neared exhaustion.

"Can . . . they . . . climb?" Conan managed.

"Not . . . well," Tull said, his voice almost a gasp.

"Good. Turn to the right."

This last phrase came as the two reached a fork in the tunnel. If Conan's memory served, they had already taken that tunnel once and circled back, and there was a rather sheer wall leading up to a narrow ledge not far ahead. Several boulders lay upon that ledge, itself four or five times the height of a tall man.

True to his recall, the steep wall loomed ahead. Conan, who had long since sheathed his blade for more efficient running, pointed at the wall. "There! Climb!"

Tull needed no clarification, and neither did he waste his breath on answering. He merely nodded once.

The pair reached the wall and began to ascend. Conan, whose early years had been spent in the cold clime and jagged peaks of Cimmeria, could climb anything that offered even the smallest of grip for his fingers. Within a few heartbeats he was to the ledge. Tull, for all his advanced age and lack of practice, arrived upon the ledge not far behind Conan. Climb or die seemed to bestow a certain skill upon the older man that Conan had not suspected.

"Now . . . what?" Tull managed between labored breaths. "We are trapped, even though they cannot reach us."

Conan, already moving toward a boulder twice the size of his head, said, "Perhaps not. A hard enough rain might persuade them to leave."

Tull took Conan's intent quickly and moved toward a slightly smaller rock.

Below, the four squirming guards rattled against the cliff's face. One of them began scraping part of his underbelly over a flat patch of rock. In a moment Conan realized that the sound thus produced was a fair counterfeit for speech.

"C-c-come d-d-down!" the scraping seemed to say. The language was one Conan had heard in Hyperborea several years past, and its meaning was clear enough.

Lifting the rock over his head, Conan leaned over the edge of the shelf upon which he and Tull stood, and hurled the rock down upon the worms.

The boulder hit the worm nearest the cliff, and the sound of the rock smashing the worm was most satisfying. Dark icteroid fluid sprayed and oozed from the crushed flesh, and the beast flailed about in its death throes.

Tull's rock also found its mark, bouncing from a second worm and doing less damage but enough to ensure the worm's demise. This one jittered madly to and fro before slowing to a post-death nervous quiver halfway across the width of the cave.

The remaining pair of worms withdrew to what they must have considered a safe distance. Conan found another rock nearly as large as the first he had thrown, and hurled it at them. The rock missed, but its path was beyond where they lay, and both worms hastily retreated past the point where the rock had impacted.

After appearing to confer for a moment, one of the worms wiggled back and forth over the rocky floor, sending another message to Conan and Tull.

"W-e-we'll b-b-be b-back!"

With that, the two turned and slithered away.

"What do you think?" Tull asked, watching as the worms vanished into the tunnel.

Conan shrugged. "Gone for help, perhaps. Or they have remembered their primary duty is to guard the witch's chambers. It matters not. Come, let us depart."

With that, Conan descended, Tull standing guard with an uplifted rock until the younger man was down. Conan drew his sword and watched while Tull clambered down the rock face. The worms did not reappear.

"I hope the girl and the idiot have had sufficient time," Tull said.

"Aye. They have had all we can supply. Let us get to the meeting place."

The main problem for Elashi and Lalo proved to be an embarrassment of riches: had they a pack animal, they could have loaded it with booty until it staggered from the weight. The witch's tenure in the caves had produced quite an accumulation of precious stones. Though it was difficult to tell precisely in the greenish light, there appeared to be rubies, emeralds, diamonds, sapphires, fire agates, opals, and pearls, according to Lalo, who claimed to have knowledge of such things.

As they gathered the valuable gems, the pair divided them into four leather sacks for easier distribution and carrying once they rejoined Conan and Tull.

Finally Elashi said, "Enough."

"But there is so much more!"

"The leather of the bags is soggy and partially

rotted," she said, "and if we overfill them, we are apt to burst the sacks."

"A valid point, for a woman. Let us depart, then."

Each of them picked up two head-sized sacks of gems and moved toward the exit. Not a moment too soon, they discovered, for as they left the witch's chambers and hurried along the corridor, a pair of worms approached from the opposite direction. Fortunately, the worms did not appear to see Elashi and Lalo as the latter pair ducked around the corner.

"This adventure is turning out much better than I expected," Lalo observed.

"Perhaps," Elashi said, "but we are not finished yet. Best you save your self-congratulations until they are more justified."

Lalo looked at Elashi with his ubiquitous smile. "Could it be that you have been cursed in the same manner as I, lady dear?"

"Listen, fool—wait! What's that?"

There came the sounds of someone approaching.

"Quick, over there!" Lalo pointed to a cleft in the rock, darkened by the lack of glow-fungus. The two of them scurried to the small opening and squatted to enter it. Once inside, they turned to observe the corridor.

A moment later a giant worm entered their view, holding by some means a rope, the other end of which was attached to a cyclops' wrists. It appeared that the worm had made a captive of the one-eyed giant.

Elashi watched the odd pair pass, but she kept part of her attention on Lalo. Sure enough, the smiling man took a deep breath and began to open his lips as if to call out an insult. Quickly the desert woman dropped one bag and clamped her hand over Lalo's mouth. Whatever sound he might have made was lost in his startlement.

The worm and the cyclops passed and moved out of sight.

Elashi removed her hand from Lalo's mouth.

"For an incredibly assertive, nay—a *pushy* woman—you have some virtue," he said.

That was as close to a compliment as Elashi had ever heard him make. She grinned in return.

"Come on. We must find Conan and Tull."

Deek and Wikkell arrived at the entrance to the witch's chambers to be met by a pair of very agitated guard worms. Wikkell stood silently by while the three worms communicated with each other in a language almost inaudible to the cyclops. After a short while Deek tugged on the rope, and he and Wikkell went into the chambers.

Once far enough away that the guards could not hear, Wikkell spoke. "What was that all about?"

"T-t-trouble f-for th-the w-w-witch. T-two of th-the m-m-men ap-appeared h-here. F-four g-g-guards g-g-gave ch-chase."

"Four guards? I only say the two."

"Th-the o-others a-are d-d-dead. Th-the m-m-men d-dropped r-r-rocks on th-them."

"How grisly." Wikkell pondered it for a moment. "Then again, this serves our purposes. Sorry about your brothers, but certainly this will not add to the witch's stature."

"T-t-true."

Wikkell looked around. "You know this place better than I. What shall we steal?"

"O-o-over h-here."

Wikkell followed the worm toward a chest of drawers. As he did, the cyclops stepped on an object sharp enough to prick even his calloused foot. He stopped and kicked the offending item from the floor. "Hmm. This is a cut gemstone. Look." He held the precious rock out for Deek to see. "Does the witch normally leave such things just laying around?"

"N-no."

Wikkell considered that for a moment. "You said the worms saw two of the men. There were others, as I recall."

"A-at l-least o-one."

"I should not wonder that while the guards chased those two, the witch might have had another visitor."

"Th-the g-g-guards a-a-re s-s-stupid. Wh-why, th-this c-c-cave is f-full o-of th-thieves!"

Wikkell laughed, and had to stop himself from becoming too loud. "Let us be about our business, Deek old slug. Find us something we can use to keep our necks—you do have a neck?—safe."

Nineteen

The Harskeel arrived near the witch's quarters in time to see a giant worm leading a cyclops bound at the wrists from the chamber, past two larger worms apparently standing guard. Moving back out of sight, the Harskeel called to Red for an explanation.

"You walk too slowly," Red said. "The men have gone."

The Harskeel ground its teeth together. "Where?"

"Not far. Two of them move to an apparent rendezvous with the two others. According to my scouts, the first pair led the guard worms away while the second pair entered the witch's chambers and later emerged carrying several bags."

The Harskeel shook its head. Thieves, and bold ones, to risk the witch's domain. Not that it mattered. It would have whatever had been stolen after it had the four slain. Which ought to happen soon, could the bats be believed.

"Which way?" the Harskeel inquired.

"Follow me," Red said.

Conan and Tull had been waiting at the rendevouz point but a few moments when Elashi and Lalo arrived, each bearing two bulging sacks.

"Amazing," Lalo said. "I thought it certain you two would have become lost and never found this spot."

Tull ground his teeth, but Conan only smiled. "I see your venture was successful."

"Enough gems to buy a kingdom," Elashi said. "And I shall allow you to carry my share." She thrust the two leather sacks at Conan.

The big Cimmerian smiled and shook his head. "I would rather keep my sword arm free," he said. "Just perchance I should need it." He took one of the sacks from her and hefted it. Unfortunately, the rotted leather, unable to withstand this movement, chose that moment to burst, spilling jewels in a glittering torrent upon the rocky floor.

"Now look what you have done!" Elashi said.

Conan did not bother to respond verbally. He merely squatted and gathered up a large handful of the fallen stones and tucked them into his belt pouch. Then he stood.

"What of the rest?" Tull asked, gesturing at the valuable gems strewn over the floor.

"I have all I can comfortably carry," Conan said.

"As Elashi has pointed out to me endlessly, there is no point in being greedy, if such makes one stupid."

"But all that wealth—"

"—will be worthless unless we escape these caves. Should I be attacked, I would not have my abilities impeded by wealth or anything else."

"Look," Lalo said, pointing. "One of the bats."

Conan glanced at the creature, which quickly flitted back the way it had come and out of sight. "One is no threat but there may be others," he said. "Best we depart." With that, he turned and started off.

Tull, Elashi, and Lalo stared at the fallen gems for a moment, then reluctantly followed the outlander. Elashi bent and retrieved a particularly large emerald-cut stone that glittered up at her. Catching up to Conan, she offered him the gem. "This one seemed too good to leave," she said.

Conan looked at the stone. Aye, it was a fine specimen. He took the jewel from her. For a moment it seemed to tingle in his fingers with a kind of subtle vibration. He tucked it into his pouch and thought no more about it.

The witch's ensorceled insect returned to her, bearing the news that the wizard moved in the opposite direction and at a goodly speed. This did not appeal to Chuntha in the least. Blast him! Both he and her prey seemed to have a head start that might well prove too great for her to make up, given the top speed of her worm raft.

Well, no problem was insurmountable. In this case, there was a way, albeit a somewhat dangerous one, to gain an advantage. Chuntha had held back on utilizing the method earlier, since the risk to her was considerable, but now it seemed the time had come for different measures. Already more dangerous conditions had arisen in the caves than ever she had faced before, and she might as well try something risky to salvage whatever she could ere there was nothing left to save.

Chuntha caused her living raft to move to a gently sloping shore with such speed that it partially beached itself. Utilizing her magic, she dissolved the spell holding the worm assemblage together, freeing her thralls into individuals once again.

"Return to my chambers as best and as quickly as you can," she ordered them.

When the worms had moved off, searching for connective tunnels that might lead them home, the witch removed from her packet of spells one she had used but once in the last two hundred years. The parchment upon which the spell was inked had been made from the scaled skin of a flying reptile thought long extinct from the world of men. This creature had been one of the last of its kind, discovered in a hidden valley deep in the fetid jungles east of Xuchotl, in the Black Kingdoms far to the south. The wingspan of such a beast dwarfed that of the largest known bird, save that of the roc; the toothed head resembled that of a crocodile; and the curved, black talons on its feet were like unto knife blades.

When the spell's words were properly uttered, the parchment would become a cloak; this cloak, when wrapped around one, metamorphically changed the wearer into a near-exact replica of that toothed and winged reptile. Fearsome and fierce, this soaring monster need fear no earthly nemesis; unfortunately, the spell had a major flaw that was its danger: one could not know how long the magical cloak would remain in effect. It might stay complete until the wearer shrugged it off hours, or even days, later; too, the cloak could fail abruptly after a few minutes and its hapless occupant might find him- or herself high above the ground, but suddenly having lost the ability to fly. Such a hazard required judicious use of the spell; failure at a sufficient height would occur but once.

Despite her varied repertoire of magics, Chuntha had only this one spell that would allow her to fly. She could not effect a means of slowing her descent should the cloak suddenly lose its effectiveness. There was one rather complex conjuration that would lighten her body to featherweight, but by the time she could intone the first few words of it, she would likely be a bloody mush upon the ground. Still, it was better to die trying as not.

The witch selected a high, rocky spire and began to climb it, carrying only the reptilian parchment with her. The ancient beings had flown and soared beyond compare, they had not done so well on ascent from the ground, so Chuntha deemed it best that she begin her flight from a high glide.

At the top of the spire she squatted and unrolled the scaled parchment, then began to read aloud the magic words.

Katamay Rey could not say that he was totally pleased with his situation, but he felt a certain confidence. A report from one of his search wasps had given him the knowledge that the witch floated on her worm raft far behind him. By the time she understood her error, both Rey and their mutual quarry should be far outside her grasp.

Only moments later, however, a strange shadow passed over the wizard. He glanced up, but the air under the high ceiling appeared empty. No, wait . . . there, ahead . . . what was that? Before he could do more than wonder, the shadowy figure was gone, leaving the wizard to surmise.

"What was that?" he said aloud.

The nearest cyclops, who had noted his master's attention and looked up, shrugged. "A bat, perhaps?"

" 'Twould be the largest one ever," Rey said. "I think not." But, he thought to himself, if not a bat, then what?

Perhaps the apparition meant nothing. Perhaps it held no threat to him. Or perhaps it was merely a figment of his imagination. But deep in his black heart, Rey felt another dagger-stab of worry.

Deek and Wikkell were feeling very pleased with themselves. The first part of the plan had gone as smoothly as a baby worm's topside. The two of them now had tucked away in Wikkell's belt a magical implement from the witch's armory. At the first clear patch of rock far enough from Chuntha's quarters to avoid arousing undue inter-est, the pair halted and Deek explained its operation.

The device looked like nothing so much as a thick chunk of wood the size of a human's playing card with a tiny hole in one end and a small lever on its side.

"P-p-point i-it a-at th-the w-w-wall o-over th-there and p-p-push th-the l-lever," Deek said.

Wikkell did so, and the thing spat a fine strand of white thread into the still air. The thread's end touched the wall, and more and more of the silky line followed, assembling itself into a bizarre tangle that formed a cobwebby net. Wikkell moved the lever back to its original position and the flow ceased abruptly, breaking contact with the magical object.

Wikkell was not altogether impressed. "So? It makes a spider's web. That is hardly much help to us."

"T-t-try to m-m-move th-through i-i-it."

Wikkell did so and quickly became entangled. His struggles only entrapped him more, until after a moment he could hardly move at all.

"All right, I am impressed. How do I get out of this?"

"R-r-reverse th-the l-l-lever."

Wikkell managed to do so. The spidery mess began to flow back into the little block of wood. Within a few moments the stuff had all disappeared, leaving the cyclops free to move again.

"I-it i-is n-n-not th-the m-m-most p-powerful sp-spell," Deek said, "b-but a-an-anyone c-can o-operate it, i-it r-requires n-no sp-special kn-knowledge."

"A distinct advantage," Wikkell observed. "Can we do so well at the wizard's quarters, I should think we could mount a powerful argument to our people."

"Th-then l-l-let u-us pr-proceed."

The two of them did just that.

*   *   *

The Harskeel could smell success. One of the bats had only just returned with the information that those whom it sought were but a few moments' walk ahead. The temptation was to hurry, but the Harskeel did not wish anything to spoil its chances. Better to proceed carefully, then attack at the most propitious moment.

As the Harskeel crossed a wide patch of rocky floor, it chanced to glance down at the pebbles that littered the area. Odd, how they glittered in this cursed green light. It bent and fetched up one of the stones.

Surprised, the Harskeel stopped and stared at the rock. Aye, rock it was, but hardly one that should be casually found upon a cavern floor. Unless it missed its guess—unlikely, since the Harskeel had some knowledge of gemology—this jewel, easily the size of its little fingertip, was nothing less than a finely cut ruby.

Further examination showed that the majority of the stones scattered at its feet were also various gems of no small value. Never one to pass up wealth for little work, the Harskeel allowed that it could pause in its chase long enough to collect the valuable minerals. His prey must have dropped them unknowingly, for certainly no one would deliberately leave such objects behind. It would take but a moment or two, and surely the Harskeel could spare that much time.

High in the vaults of the dark cave, a giant creature soared on leathery wings, flying with great speed and grace, hurrying to arrive at its destination before the magic that kept it aloft ceased working.

Inside the cloak, Chuntha felt the power of the thing whose kind had ruled the air millions of years before men lived on the earth. It was most seductive, the feeling of flight . . . the sensual nature of it could easily become addictive. The risk, however, outweighed the thrill for her. There were better ways to achieve warm feelings than to chance the final dance with death.

As soon as she collected her barbarian, the witch thought, she would show one of those ways to him. True, he would not survive the encounter, but ah, he would enjoy his final moments of ecstasy . . .

Twenty

As Conan led his friends down a winding tunnel with a high ceiling, something most strange happened. Behind him, Lalo said, "I fear yon lout leads us to certain doom."

This insult was but one of a more or less constant stream of similar comments, and Conan had begun to learn how to ignore them. Only this time there came another sentence almost immediately upon the heels of the statement, as if it were an echo: *But would that I were Conan and ready to face whatever might come with no more than a sword and his courage.*

Conan paused and turned to Lalo. "What was that?"

"Pray what is the matter, Conan? Are your ears plugged, so that you are now deaf as well as harebrained?"

And again the voice softly followed: *Would that I could speak my admiration of you, Conan, and not be forced to vilify you with every passing moment.*

It came to Conan then that the voice he heard, which was most definitely that of Lalo, had not reached him through his hearing but had arisen from within his head, much as the voice of the Webspinner had done earlier.

"Nothing, never mind," Conan said, turning back to the path ahead. What sorcery was this? He had heard Lalo speak, but he was certain that the speech within his head was in fact what the grinning man was truly thinking when he had made the rude comment.

Something was definitely amiss were that the case, but Conan thought it prudent to avoid mentioning it; perhaps he was simply imagining things.

A few moments later, as Elashi negotiated a steep spot on the cavern floor, she slipped and fell, landing solidly but unhurt upon her ample backside. Her cloak and undershift slid well back, revealing her slim legs almost to their juncture. Conan admired the view.

Elashi looked up and saw Conan smiling at her. "Goat," she said. "Can you think of nothing else?"

But following her speech came that eerie voice in Conan's mind again: *Ah, would that we had a few moments to be alone together, Conan, my ram. All of this excitement has stirred my lusts.*

Conan blinked, certain that the others must have heard her, but it seemed apparent from their demeanor that neither Tull nor Lalo had caught the second portion of Elashi's speech. Or, Conan was convinced, her thoughts.

How could he hear these things? Had some kind of spell been cast upon him?

Upon reflection, that made no sense he could discern. What would be the purpose of such a geas? Certainly it was to his advantage, not to that of any of his opponents. To know what a man or a woman thought, whatever they might say, was a powerful tool.

Well. That it had happened seemed the important thing. Worry about how or why could be left for when there was more time to ponder upon the cause. If you were tethered by a thick rope and a man handed you a sharp blade, you did not bother yourself with the origin of the iron or the name of the smith who had made it; you cut yourself free.

Conan was nothing if not pragmatic.

And perhaps it would be better not to mention this new talent to the others just yet.

"They are just ahead," Red said to the Harskeel. "All four of them, around that next turning."

"Are your fellows ready to attack?"

"We would have an end to this and receive our promised bloodspell. Yes, we are ready."

"Good. Then let us finish this unpleasant business."

The Harskeel increased its speed toward the turning, not more than twenty paces distant.

*   *   *

Still draped in the mantle of the flying reptile, Chuntha alighted in front of her quarters and the two startled guard worms.

They shied away, until she removed the magical cloak long enough to show them who she was.

The worms looked vastly relieved. The leader reported their encounter with the barbarian. "H-he m-m-must b-be a d-demon! He s-s-slew C-c-cook and T-t-tuma!"

She waved the two worms to silence. The loss of two guards was nothing; the important thing was that the barbarian was nearby. No time to stop and rest, then.

She did not ask of further matters.

The witch climbed onto the tail of the larger guard. "When I change back into the winged creature, you are to use your muscles to hurl me into the air, that way," she said, pointing. Without waiting for a reply, Chuntha donned the scaled garment and once again assumed the form of its former owner.

The startled guard, no less so for having been told this would happen, lashed his tail sharply, catapulting the ensorceled witch into the air like a rock hurled from a sling. The leathery wings fluttered and snapped out, and Chuntha sailed down the long corridor.

There were several ways the barbarian could have taken, but she knew at least one that he had not and others that were less than likely. She was near, she felt it, and she would have him soon!

Katamay Rey had long since attained the shore, and now his cyclopian carriers bore him in a jolting run down the most direct corridor toward home. He had the distinct feeling of being late to the party, and tardiness in this case might well be his undoing.

"Hurry, you useless lumps, hurry!"

If anything, the continuation of Wikkell and Deek's plan went smoother than had the beginning. The pair of cyclopes who guarded Rey's chambers knew better than to impede Wikkell's comings and goings; apparently the wizard had not bothered to enlighten them as to Wikkell's current status, an oversight that the cyclops had counted upon. The wizard thought they were all morons, and seldom bothered to inform the cyclops of anything that did not directly concern them. Wikkell knew that Rey also thought that little, if any, of his business concerned anyone save himself, so the fear that the guards would attempt to stop Wikkell had been a small worry at best.

With Deek slithering along behind him on the leash, the two of them entered the wizard's chambers.

As they had done in the witch's quarters, the rogue cyclops and renegade worm quickly selected a talisman and departed. Once away from the general vicinity of the guards, it was Wikkell's turn to demonstrate to Deek the instrument they had just stolen.

It seemed to Deek that the small graystone jar was innocuous enough. From it Wikkell removed a pinch of pale powder and cast it in a glittery shower upon the floor before the worm.

"Wh-what d-d-does i-it d-d-do?"

"Crawl over it and see."

Had he shoulders, Deek would have shrugged; lacking them, he twisted his body slightly and started to slither over the fine power. Quickly the worm found that he could not gain any purchase on the floor. He could move his own body by contracting his muscles, but there was no friction between his body and the underlying rock. It was as if the solid stone had turned to air for all the resistance it offered.

Wikkell grinned down at his friend. "A special lubricant," he said. "You cannot move upon a surface coated with it, nor can anybody do anything but slip and slide upon it. Here."

With that, Wikkell leaned toward Deek and gave him a gentle shove. Deek slid across the rock more easily than had their web boat over the surface of the water. He hit a patch of normal rock half a body length behind, and hastened to inch himself back onto it.

"Im-im-impressive," Deek said. "I-is i-it p-p-permanent?"

"No. It lasts but an hour or so, then vanishes. Still, with these two items to show our brethren, perhaps we can generate more support."

"Un-un-d-doubtedly."

"Then let us waste no more time. My folk or yours?"

"M-m-mine a-a-are cl-closer."

"Then lead on, friend."

Conan's sharp hearing caught the high-pitched sound of the chittering bats before his companions noted their approach. The Cimmerian wheeled about, drawing his sword and frightening the others with the suddenness of his movement.

"Conan—what—?" Elashi began.

"Bats, behind us!" Conan said.

The bats, more than a dozen strong, boiled through the green light toward them. They were in a fairly wide cave, though it had begun to narrow where Conan and the others stood. A few more paces and they could attain a short tunnel that would force the oncoming bats to fly in tandem to enter it.

Tull pulled his knife and Elashi her sword, while Lalo bent for a fist-sized rock.

"Into the tunnel," Conan ordered. "I shall hold them until you are inside."

"Conan—" Elashi began.

"Do as I say, quickly!"

The three obeyed, and Conan could hear the fear in their thoughts, along with their reluctance to leave him alone to face the bats. They had no intention of deserting him, and he smiled grimly at the power of knowing their minds. He raised his sword for the first cut.

The first bat to arrive felt the shock of cold iron slicing through him but realized his mistake too late. Entrails spilled as the dying creature careened into a stalagtite and expired.

The second and third attackers fared no better as a backstroke with the sharped blue iron took one's head from its furry shoulders and the return stroke sheared the hindquarters from the other.

There were too many of them, though. Before Conan could ready the sword for another cut, four of the bats barreled into him. They were much smaller and lighter than he, but the weight and momentum of their number were enough to knock him from his feet. He stabbed upward as he fell, skewering one of the bats.

One of the other attackers dragged its claws over Conan's shoulder, drawing blood to fill the gouges. Conan grabbed the thing's neck with his free hand and squeezed. Small bones and cartilage cracked wetly as the Cimmerian tossed the strangled bat away from him.

Behind the frantic fluttering of the bats, Conan saw the form of the Harskeel. He might have suspected that one was still around.

The Harskeel darted toward Conan, a thin blade drawn for action, but it could not get close enough to bring its blade into play—the flurry of bats darting hither and yon impeded it.

Behind him, Conan heard Tull, Elashi, and Lalo yell.

"We are coming, Conan!"

As Conan punched one of the bats square in the face with his knotted fist, shattering that poor creature's teeth and jaw, he thought that the odds now seemed more in their favor. A few more bats, one man; they could deal with those—

Something screamed.

It was an unearthly sound, like nothing the Cimmerian had ever heard; a grating, screeching roar that made the skin of his neck chill and bump. It came from above, that horrible shriek. He risked a glance upward and noticed that the bats and the Harskeel did the same.

A flying monster swooped down toward him. It had a long, thin head and a mouth filled with teeth the size of a man's fingers, and its wings seemed to stretch halfway across the breadth of the cave.

Conan jerked his sword back to strike at the thing—Crom, it was huge!—but one of the bats, trying to get away from the descending horror, flitted behind him just as the Cimmerian cocked the blade and started to shift his grip on the handle. The edge of the blued iron bit into the bat's skull, effectively stopping further voluntary activity by the bat; unfortunately, the blade stuck in the wet bone, and the weight of the bat was enough to pull the sword from a startled Conan's too-loose grip.

Time to leave, Conan thought. He turned to sprint toward his friends, but it was too late. The talons of the flying monster closed upon him, one claw gripping his arm like an iron band, the other snagging in the leather of his belt. Conan felt himself lifted into the air as easily as a newborn child picked up by its mother. The flapping of the great wings fanned the air, stirring up a stinging spray of rocky grit and mold from the cavern floor.

"Run!" Conan yelled to his friends.

In answer, Lalo took aim and hurled his rock. Unfortunately, his aim was less than perfect and the rock struck Conan on the thigh.

"Go!" Conan yelled.

Conan was already too high for his friends to reach. They needed no further urging. The three of them ran for the small exit tunnel as Conan was lifted yet higher into the air by the demonic flying beast.

Beneath him, the Harskeel screamed in a voice

that started deep but quickly rose to a woman's shrillness. "Noooooo!"

The monster bearing Conan banked to the left and flapped away. Conan did not struggle. To be dropped from this altitude upon the rocky floor could hardly help his cause. Better to see where this thing would end its flight than to be dashed to jelly upon the surface below.

The Harskeel's rage evaporated in an instant as it realized that which had dropped upon it from the monster above was none other than Conan's blood. Only a few drops, to be sure, but certainly that would be enough? And the sword lay embedded in one of the dead bats on the ground, not three paces away!

The Harskeel had started for the fallen sword when Red alighted upon the floor in its path.

"Stand aside," the Harskeel ordered.

"We are done trucking with you," Red said, fluttering his wings in apparent anger. "Give us our spell, now!"

"Certainly, certainly, in a moment. I only need fetch that— "

"Now!"

It was too much. To be thwarted by a fool of a bat when its goal lay within reach was too much. The Harskeel whipped its blade around in a flat arc, all the strength of its shoulder and upper arm in the blow. Red's head spewed blood as it looped through the air and fell, to bounce twice upon the cavern floor.

There were perhaps five or six bats still uninjured. They glanced at one another, then at the Harskeel.

"Anyone else in a hurry?"

No one, it seemed, was in a hurry.

The Harskeel walked to Conan's fallen blade and wrenched it free of the dead bat. The words of the spell came to it, firmly set in its memory after all the years of searching. The few drops of Conan's blood were carefully scraped onto the tip of the blue iron, and the point of the sword was just as carefully drawn down the Harskeel's body by its trembling hands, making a thin furrow from the top of its head to its crotch.

The last words of the spell came from the Harskeel's throat.

The air around it began to shimmer, and the Harskeel felt a surge of joy. It was going to work! Already it could feel itself—no, *them*selves—begin to separate into two beings. The male half focused on the right, the female half on the left, as the furrow—drawn by the blade and the blood of a truly brave man—combined with the magic of the spell to widen, forming two people where before there had been one.

The remaining bats watched in awe. The Harskeel laughed, the sound now coming from two throats and two mouths. Success! It had killed hundreds, slain indiscriminately, robbed, cheated, stolen, and finally, finally after all the years, it had achieved its—no, not its—*their* goal! The lovers would now become two, as they had been before.

Stretching apart as might a strand of elastic clay, what had been split finally into two. A moment later, a man stood facing a woman. Their smiles were radiant.

"What is this?" came a voice from behind them.

The man and the woman turned. The man held Conan's blade, the woman the thin sword that had been the Harskeel's.

They found themselves facing none other than Katamay Rey.

"Who are you?" the wizard demanded to know.

"None of your affair," the woman said.

"Hold your tongue," the man standing next to her said.

"After all these years? I will not!"

"It was your hasty speech that got us into this mess originally," the man said.

"I beg your pardon! It was *you* who—"

"Silence!" the wizard yelled. "I have not the time for this bickering."

"If we are fast enough, we can take him," the woman said, dropping her voice to a whisper.

"Do not be a fool," the man whispered back.

"Now!" she yelled. The woman leaped toward the wizard, the sword held ready to cut him down. Half a step behind her, the man who had recently been joined with her managed to shake his head as he jumped to follow her. One more killing would hardly cause them problems.

A pair of cyclopes stood behind Rey, but at some distance. They would not be able to intervene in time.

The wizard raised his hands and waggled his fingers, and he spoke four hard-edged and harsh words.

Even as he gathered himself for the final leap to

chop down the wizard, the man who had been half of the Harskeel felt himself slow, as if his feet had become liquid. He chanced a quick glance down, and in an almost detached manner noted that this was indeed so—his feet *had* become fluid. Even as he looked, his lower legs sank into the puddle that had been his feet. There was no pain, but a foul odor came from the ooze.

The man twisted his body to look at the woman with whom he had been perversely intimate for so long. Her lower half now consisted of an identical ooze, and she sank rapidly into this bubbling pool of high stench, looking quite puzzled.

"Now look what you have done!" she said, her voice a wail.

"I? *I* have done?"

It was the man's last speech, and in a moment the words were followed by his final thought: curse all the gods!

An instant later the two who had been the Harskeel of Loplain were nothing but bubbling puddles of stinking slime upon the floor of the cave.

Twenty-one

Deek's appearance accompanied by a cyclops caused no small stir amongst his kind.

"—D-d-deek! Wh-wh-what i-is th-this—?"

"—h-h-how c-came y-you b-by on-one-eye—?"

"—a-are y-you c-crazy—?"

But a short demonstration that first ensnared some of their folk and then turned the floor to oiled ice beneath others of them stirred them even more.

"—b-by all the g-g-gods—!"

"—r-r-remove th-th-this st-stuff—!"

"Think they are ready to listen?" Wikkell asked.

"S-so it w-w-would s-s-seem."

So the worms listened as Deek and Wikkell out-

lined their scheme. While there was no general-
ized rush to mount a revolution against the witch,
voices that had been still before now were heard.
That there was dissatisfaction with Chuntha's rule
no one doubted; that there might be a chance to
void that rule had never been thought likely. But if
all of the giant worms joined with all of the cyclopes,
perhaps such a thing *was* possible. Deek and
Wikkell's possession of the two talismans they had
purloined indicated that the witch and the wizard
did indeed have vulnerable spots.

The discussion heated up and the talks were not
short; in the end, though, the worms reached a
consensus: if Deek and Wikkell could guarantee
participation by the one-eyes, well, then, certainly
the worms would be willing to fight alongside of
them.

Deek and Wikkell looked at each other, and each
knew the jubilation the other must feel. Success!

Well, to be sure, it was only half successful; still,
with the worms' promise in hand, they had a potent weapon to sway the cyclopes to their argument.

Leaving the worms' chambers, Deek and Wikkell
went to visit the cyclopes.

As his captor flew through the caves on its huge,
leathery wings, Conan wondered which of the two
magical rulers was responsible for his plight. That
either the witch or the wizard had sent this beast
was apparent. And it also seemed that he was
wanted alive, else he would surely be dead by
now. The flying monster merely had to loosen its
grip and allow the fall to do the deed.

The answer to the Cimmerian's question was

not long in coming. That tickle of words inside Conan's head came again: *We shall be home soon, my beautiful barbar.*

Definitely female, that voice, and since it seemed to come from the toothed reptile carrying him, Conan figured that the witch was somehow within the form of the creature.

Indeed. As the cave's walls seemed to close in and the floor grew closer, the thing holding him turned and swooped down familiar tunnels, reaching at last the entrance to Chuntha's chambers. Two large worms stood guard over the portal. Conan could not be certain that those two were the same he had seen before, since all of the worms looked alike to him, but he suspected it was so.

The creature settled to the floor, loosing its grip on the Cimmerian but remaining within the reach of the worms. A hasty move might be repaid with a slap of one of those massive tails, and Conan did not desire to discover how powerful such a stroke might be.

Any thoughts of quick escape fled when the scaled reptile suddenly altered its shape. After a shimmer in the air, Conan beheld the form of the witch for the first time. He had expected a crone, wrinkled and crusty, bent with ages of evil, speaking in a cracked and raspy cackle, but that was not what he beheld, not at all.

Crom, she was beautiful! And naked! Her face, her breasts, her long and well-formed legs, her dark, silky hair . . . everything about her was altogether lovely.

The witch's smile was sensual and full of invitation.

"I have been searching for you for too long a time," she said. "We have much to . . . discuss."

Conan stared at the naked woman. Surely a woman who looked like this could not be as bad as he had been led to believe?

"Come," she said. "Into my chambers. You must be tired from your fight with the bats. You can lie down on my bed and . . . relax."

Relaxing was not high upon Conan's list of desired activities at the moment. Hardly. A man could not stand next to such a woman and think of rest, save in the most abstract of futures. Rest? Later. Much later. Added to his thoughts came the feathery touch of that mindspeech he had begun to hear recently: *We shall lie together on my bed, strong one, and I shall show you pleasure beyond any you have ever known.*

Chuntha turned, and the view from behind was as lovely as that from the front. Conan watched her walk away. Actually, it was more of sway than a walk, and the muscles moved under her smooth and silky skin in a most interesting manner.

Without prompting, Conan followed. He seemed to recall Tull's warnings about the witch, but the memory was dim and distant compared to the reality of the woman he beheld.

The escape tunnel that Tull, Elashi, and Lalo had chosen was instead a dead end. It stopped abruptly at a flat wall, and there was no option save to turn around and retrace their steps.

The three had not gone a dozen paces, however,

when they halted again. A pair of cyclopes stood there, blocking the exit. After a moment the cyclopes moved apart, revealing just behind them the form of Katamay Rey.

"Ah, my friends," the wizard said. "You left so abruptly earlier that we did not have time to finish our discussion. And look, another has joined you." Rey nodded at Lalo. "Have I not seen you somewhere before?"

"I have only just dropped in," Lalo said, ever smiling.

"Mm. Of course, I recall. Sent by Chuntha, were you?"

"Not at all, you pea-brained fool."

Startled, the wizard raised one hand, then stopped. "There's something about you ... ah, I have it! You are enspelled. My brother Mambaya Rey used to have such a curse at his disposal. Perhaps you know him?"

For once Lalo was struck with silence.

"Well, no matter, no matter. I see that your large companion has left you. Where is he?"

None of the three spoke.

The wizard grinned. "Ah, well, we can discuss this more at our leisure back at my chambers. You will come and visit, will you not?" He waved at the cyclopes flanking him, and they moved toward the three.

Tull and Elashi glanced at each other, and Tull shook his head. A knife and a sword would be of little use against these, and Lalo's wrestling less so. They were captured. Conan was gone. Things did not look good.

*   *   *

Wikkell's people seemed at first a bit more skeptical than had Deek's; still, the presence of the giant worm added to their interest.

"Talk is cheap, brother," one of the cyclopes said.

"Indeed," Wikkell replied. He lifted the web device and pointed it at the doubting cyclops. The thin spray shot forth.

"Hey!"

In a moment the doubting one was so entangled he could not move, save to squirm.

"Help me!"

When half a dozen others moved to do so, Wikkell turned the floor into perfect smoothness, and the six slipped and fell and slid hither and yon.

"W-w-we s-seem to h-have g-gotten their a-attention."

"Yes, we have, haven't we?"

Several hours later the discussions came to their conclusion. Yes, the cyclopes would join the worms in overthrowing the witch and the wizard. What exactly was the plan? How was it to be instigated?

Wikkell drew himself up and said, "Deek and I have that all arranged. First you are to choose a war council, with leaders. The worms shall do the same, and the two of us will then present our plan to the leaders of both sides at once, to save repetition. Naturally, Deek and I intend to be commanders of our respective troops."

With that, Wikkell marched away, Deek following. The murmur of the cyclopes as they began to vie for position trailed the two down the corridor.

At a distance at which they would not be overheard, Deek found a patch of speech rock. "Wh-

what p-p-plan? Th-this i-is th-the f-f-first I-I have h-heard o-of s-s-such a p-p-plan!"

"I had to say something, did I not? Frankly, I felt all along that our chances of ever getting this far were remote at best. I never really believed that we should actually have to mount a war against the witch and the wizard."

"W-w-well, w-we h-h-have c-come t-to i-it. N-n-now wh-what a-are w-we t-to d-d-do?"

"Devise a plan of attack, it would seem. Got any ideas?"

"I-I a-am b-beginning t-t-to r-regret I w-was e-ever h-h-hatched," Deek said. If it is possible for the body of a worm scraping over rock to intone regret, the voice thus produced indeed sounded regretful.

"Cheer up, Deek old slug. We are no worse off than we were before. Who knows? We might even win."

"I-I sh-shall n-not w-w-wager m-my n-n-nest o-on th-that p-p-possibility."

The witch proceeded to a large bed that lay in the center of the room. She climbed onto the bed, crawled to the middle on her hands and knees, then turned and lay upon her back. She smiled at Conan. "Come here, my beautiful barbarian man. I would feel your warmth next to me."

Conan had been with more than a few women in his young life, but none who had ever called to him quite like this. His mouth was dry as he started for the bed.

Came the mindspeech: *Come and enjoy total pleasure, big man, and give me your strength. It will be your finest thrill, and your last.*

Conan paused at that. His last?

"Why do you keep me waiting? Am I not desirable?"

Spend your manly essence within me, and with it your life force. Hurry, I hunger for it!

Conan continued to move toward the woman—she was no less beautiful and enticing than before—but a note of caution sounded within him. This mindspeech was the truth, not the words she spoke, and he realized that to consummate his lust with this creature—who was, after all, a witch—would be his death knell. But what was he to do? She desired him, and were he to thwart that desire, there was no foretelling what she might turn to next. An ordinary woman scorned was dangerous; what evil might a witch refused do him?

What was it she had said? She wanted his essence? Well, if he could somehow manage to avoid doing what she wanted, then perhaps he had a chance to survive.

How to manage that was another matter altogether. Death was an expensive price to pay for a few moments of pleasure. Crom would hardly welcome a man who would make such a foolish trade. This manner of combat was scarcely comparable to dying in battle with a sword in hand.

Conan searched for memories of ice and snow, and wading through freezing water.

Such thoughts helped but little.

"You are quite lovely," Rey told Elashi.

The desert woman stood next to Tull and Lalo. The wizard had taken their weapons, and they all were now inside his personal chamber. A pair of cyclopes waited just outside the door.

"I have had no need for women for some years," Rey continued, "but I might rekindle the old fires for one such as you."

"I would rather be boiled in oil than suffer your attentions," Elashi said.

"What?"

"Are your ears stuffed with mold?" Lalo asked. "The lady finds you repellent, a feeling in which I concur wholeheartedly."

"Cannot you two keep silent?" Tull said, his voice low. "You do not want to make him angry. He is very powerful."

"Wise," Rey said. "You will have a quick death for that. These other two will suffer a bit longer, after they have told me the whereabouts of whatever his name is . . . Conan?"

"I expect Conan is long gone from these caves and safe from either you or the witch," Elashi said.

"Would that it were so," Rey said, "for he is dangerous; still, I cannot take the chance that he might yet be free down here. You will aid me in his capture, like it or not. I am not a man to be trifled with, as you shall learn."

Tull, Elashi, and Lalo looked at each other. This did not bode well. Elashi was most worried about Conan. She feared he was in dire straits indeed.

Twenty-two

"W-w-will th-the b-bats and Wh-whites d-do i-it?"

Reluctantly Wikkell turned to face Deek. They were in the cave in which the cyclopes regularly bathed. A small cataract spilled from a high ledge upon which Deek and Wikkell perched, splashing into the shallow pond below. The sound of the water covered their voices from the female cyclopes who were cavorting below them in the pond. An attractive lot, Wikkell noted, and he would certainly rather be down there with them than up here with Deek.

"W-Wikkell?"

"What? Oh, sorry, Deek. Yes, I think they will do it. I doubt that the plants will be of much use to us, but given the weight of numbers, I do not believe they will oppose us either. I expect the initial charge of the Whites and the bats might prove costly to them, but if they want to continue to live in the caves, I feel it is only right that they share the risks of our endeavor."

"O-o-one c-c-cannot m-make m-m-mushroom w-wine w-without c-c-crushing a f-few t-t-toad-stools."

"Well put, Deek. The time must be soon for our strike, are we to keep our intent secret."

Wikkell glanced back down at the female cyclopes. One of them saw him and waved. He waved back.

"S-s-someone y-you kn-know w-w-well?"

"Not yet. If we survive the upcoming confrontation, though, I hope to get to know her much better."

"A-as o-one-eyes g-go, s-she s-s-seems qu-quite l-lovely."

"I always knew you were a worm of good taste. You must introduce me to your nestmates when this is done."

"Wh-when i-it is d-d-done."

At least several hours had elapsed, although to Conan the passage of time felt more like days; finally the witch fell into what the Cimmerian hoped would be an exhausted—and long—slumber.

He had felt better himself, he thought, as he hurriedly gathered his clothes. His belt pouch fell with a thump that seemed terribly loud, and Conan froze at the sound. Several of the jewels rattled from the purse and onto the hard floor. Conan ignored them, even though one of them was the large gem than Elashi had given him.

Chuntha did not stir from her torpid pose, and the Cimmerian finished collecting his garb and quickly moved toward the cave's exit.

Conan considered the problem of the guard worms as he finished dressing. His sword lay back in the cave where he and his friends had fought the bats. A bare-handed struggle against the worms held little appeal. How was he to bypass the pair? True, they were set to guard the cave from intruders, not from one leaving. Utilizing surprise, he could most likely dart past them before they could gather their wits. By the time they recovered enough to pursue him, he would be well ahead, and he knew from his earlier experience that he could outrun the slithering beasts.

On the other hand, while such an action might gain him an immediate lead on the worms, they also might not bother to pursue him at all. The guards could just as easily enter the cave and rouse Chuntha, and Conan had considerable doubt about his ability to outrun the monstrous flying reptile into which the witch could transform herself. A dilemma.

In the end he decided that the key lay in boldness. He had recognized the speech produced by the worms and could speak a fair portion of it. He took a deep breath and stepped out through the chambers' entrance.

"Ho, guards," he said in the tongue the worm had spoken earlier.

The two worms spun around, coiling as might serpents preparing to strike.

"Chuntha slumbers and wishes to be undisturbed," Conan said. "I am being sent to fetch a thing for her. Move aside."

Conan gambled that the worms would assume his apparent nonchalance meant what he said was true. The Cimmerian doubted that many, if any, of Chuntha's guests had ever left at all, much less without her express permission, and reckoned that the guards would know this and fear to question her orders.

The two worms seemed to look at each other, though whatever organs they used that passed for eyes were not apparent to Conan. The Cimmerian suffered a long and tense moment . . .

Then, with a slight rotation that Conan took to be a shrug, the pair relaxed back into their earlier poses.

Striving to look as if he owned every inch of the caves, Conan strolled away at a leisurely pace, never looking back.

When he was around the first turning in the corridor, Conan picked up his pace considerably. He had escaped from the carnal clutches of the witch, but he still had to find his friends. He began to run, planning to put a goodly distance between himself and the witch as soon as possible.

He had been at the sprint but for a few moments when he rounded a corner and ran smack into a tangled nest of sticky webbing. He tried to back away from the clinging threads, but he could neither escape nor break free of them. The more he struggled, the more enmeshed he became. Even his powerful muscles were no match for the strength of the fibers. He was still try fruitlessly to break free when he saw a cyclops standing next to a giant worm, watching him.

What now? he thought.

"I-I-I a-am n-not s-sure a-ab-about th-this." Deek watched the man struggle against the grip of the magical webbing.

Next to Deek, Wikkell nodded as if in agreement but said, "I understand your reluctance. Still, somehow, this one is at the root of all this. Both my master and your mistress—"

"E-e-ex-m-m-master a-and m-m-mistress," Deek broke in and corrected.

"Yes, yes, to be sure. Our *ex*-master and mistress seemed to think this man was of some import. As we have seen, he certainly is resourceful. He has managed to escape from both wizard and witch on his own, no small task."

"B-b-but c-can w-we t-t-trust him?"

"I would rather have him on our side than against us. Certainly he has no more love for Rey and Chuntha than do we. And we do have something to offer, do we not?"

"Y-y-yes."

"Then let us go and speak with him."

In the wizard's chambers, Rey questioned Elashi. He had a pair of his cyclopes holding her tightly as he stood sharpening a somewhat rusted knife with a stone. The sound of the blade being whetted made cold, scraping noises in the quiet room. Tull and Lalo stood against a nearby wall, manacled to the rock. While the chains and wrist clamps were covered with thick scales of red-brown rust flakes, the iron had lost none of its core strength.

Rey finished working on the knife. He touched the edge with one thumb; apparently it was done to his satisfaction. He moved toward Elashi, grinning wickedly in the green light, and waved the knife gently back and forth as he drew nearer to the desert woman.

The two cyclopes had firm grips on both of Elashi's arms; unfortunately for Rey, both of the woman's slender but strong legs remained unencumbered. When the wizard was within her range, Elashi managed to launch a stiff kick.

"Ah!" The wizard grunted, expelling most of his air. He stumbled back to the accompaniment of congratulatory noises from Tull and Lalo for Elashi's action.

It was but a short diversion, however, and the effect of Elashi's resistance did nothing to improve Rey's mood.

"Hold her feet!" the wizard ordered when his breath had returned.

Though Elashi kicked and struggled, it was but a moment's work for the cyclopes to each capture one leg. Firmly gripped now at the upper arm and ankle, Elashi found herself held stretched horizontally between her two captors much like a blanket among players of the childhood game of "Toss the Man High and Catch Him."

Rey moved in and inserted the sharpened blade under Elashi's belt. A single jerk of his wrist sliced the leather strap, and the belt fell away. The wizard moved to the hem of her heavy fabric skirt and gripped it with one hand, cutting the material to her crotch. The skirt gaped, revealing the smooth skin of her legs all the way to her underclothes.

Two more passes with the knife and Elashi lay stretched between the cyclopes naked save for her boots. The wizard stepped between her spread legs and laid the flat of the blade knife upon her belly. "Ready to tell me where Conan is?"

"Rot in the deepest hell!" Elashi said. Her voice quivered, but she tried to keep her face impassive.

Rey turned the knife so that it was edge down. He started to press the edge into her flesh . . .

"Wait!" Lalo yelled. "I shall tell you!"

"Lalo! Say nothing!" Elashi said.

The wizard turned away from the woman. "Yes?"

Lalo's grin looked pained, and his insult when it came was weak: "Wicked fool, spare her and I shall tell you Conan's location."

"I spare no one. But I can make her death quick."

Lalo nodded. "Very well. Conan hides in a small grotto some distance away. Tull here has used it for his residence for some years."

Tull and Elashi managed to stare at Lalo with amazement and disbelief; the wizard undoubtedly thought this due to Lalo's treachery.

"Explain to me the location and you shall live until my cyclopes return with the barbarian."

Tull and Elashi caught on to Lalo's ploy.

Tull said, "Tell him nothing, you traitor!"

"I hate you!" Elashi said.

Ever-smiling, Lalo took a deep breath and began to tell the wizard how to get to Tull's grotto.

Seemingly satisfied, the wizard had Elashi chained next to the two men. She drew her tattered clothes about her as best she could and settled down upon the rocky floor, shaking from nervous reaction.

Rey swept out of the chamber to instruct his thralls in the retrieval of Conan. It was only when the wizard appeared to be well out of earshot that the three captives spoke to each other, and then in quiet whispers.

"Why did you tell him Conan was in my grotto?" Tull asked. "When last we saw him—"

"—some monster had captured the awkward oaf," Lalo finished. "Aye, and since the flying creature did not come from Rey, then we may be almost certain it was dispatched by the witch. We could have hardly told him that, now could we? 'Conan? Why, the witch has him.' That would have sealed our doom instantly, would it not?"

"Lalo is right," Elashi whispered. "At least this way we have purchased a bit more time."

"Besides," Lalo said, "I had to say something. I could not allow him to harm you."

Although Lalo's smile was perpetual with him, it seemed to soften somewhat when he said this, and Elashi grinned at him in return. "I thank you for that."

"Even as stupid and worthless as you are, you have more uses alive than dead," Lalo said. From him, this was practically a raging compliment, and Elashi shook her head from the wonder of it.

"All this is beginning to get on my nerves," Tull said. He got no argument from either of the others on that point.

"What will we do when Rey discovers that Conan is not where we said he would be?" Elashi asked.

"Try to deceive him further," Lalo whispered.

" 'Gone? Well, yes, of course. He said that if we did not meet him there soon, he would go to the waterfall where first he met Tull.' And after that, mayhap we can send him yet elsewhere."

"He is certain to catch on after a time or two. It is a decidedly risky plan," Tull said.

"Better than no plan at all," Elashi observed. "Besides, what have we to lose now?"

Another point no one wished to speak to or think overly about . . . not while chained to a cold wall in the chambers of an evil wizard.

Twenty-three

Conan saw the two figures approaching, but he was unable to offer a defense or to flee. When the unlikely pair arrived at a distance two spans from him, they stopped.

"We would speak with you," the one-eyed giant said.

The Cimmerian looked down at his trapped limbs. Bound as he was in the sticky webbing, he had no choice save to listen to the cyclops and the worm. "I am listening," he said, as if he had a choice.

"Things are not as we would have them in our realm," the cyclops said. "We intend a change."

"W-w-we n-need y-your h-h-help," the worm said.

They went on to explain what they had in mind.

While his intention was to find his friends and flee this accursed realm as soon as possible, the alternative offered by the pair certainly held merits the Cimmerian had to ponder, especially considering his current state.

"So," the cyclops said, "that is our intent. If you help us achieve it, you and your friends will be free to go on about your own business with our blessings."

"And if I do not agree?"

"W-we c-can l-leave y-y-you h-here t-to r-r-rot," the worm said in that grating speech of his.

It was, Conan had to admit, a most powerful argument.

"Well, then, I agree to aid you. Both witch and wizard have done nothing but cause me grief since I arrived here. I would see them in Gehanna at the earliest opportunity."

The cyclops, who had given his name as Wikkell, nodded and turned to the worm. "See? I told you he would be reasonable."

With that, the giant one-eyed being extended a small wooden device toward Conan and his nest of sticky threads. After a moment the threads began to pull away from Conan's body and the small block of wood somehow sucked the strings into itself. A few seconds later all of the netting in which Conan had been trapped had vanished.

Magic, and no doubt of that. He liked it not at all. Still, it was not as if he had been given much in the way of choice. Whatever the reason, he was a man of his word; once his pledge was given, he would not break it.

"Our sources tell us that your friends have been collected by the wizard," Wikkell said.

"Are they well?"

"I have it as likely . . . for as long as the wizard thinks they might lead him to you."

"Why is it that I am so important to both witch and wizard?"

"Wh-who k-knows?" This from the worm, who called himself Deek.

"I think it perhaps has something to do with some kind of prophesy," Wikkell said. "In some way, the wizard fears you, and likewise, so does the witch."

"I cannot understand why. I have no magic; I am no more than an ordinary man."

"A man, perhaps. Hardly ordinary. To have escaped from the wizard, and then from the witch after sharing her bed, these are things no man has ever done before."

"W-w-were i-it n-n-not f-for y-you, n-n-none o-of th-this w-w-would h-have h-happened."

Conan shrugged. "I think this is all due to being in the wrong place at the wrong time."

"Whatever the original reason," Wikkell said, "it does not matter so much now."

The three started down the corridor. Conan pondered what they had told him. They would aid him in freeing his friends. There was to be an attack, and during it he might be able to take advantage of the confusion. If he should happen to slay the wizard in passing? Well, so much the better.

Deek and Wikkell spoke of their actions over the last days, and Conan filled them in on his own adventures. They seemed impressed, although he told his story in an offhand manner devoid of bragging.

A few moments later several of the Blind Whites came down the rocky hallway toward Conan and the others. Conan tensed, but Wikkell quickly reassured him there was no need to worry. The Whites were now in league with the cyclopes and the worms. The witch and the wizard were about to have a full-scale revolution on their hands.

One of the Whites approached and spoke to Wikkell in a language Conan did not recognize. After a moment another of the Whites was motioned to come closer by the cyclops.

The second White carried an object over one shoulder, something Conan had not noticed earlier: his sword!

The White tendered the blade to Wikkell, who held it as a man would hold a long knife. The cyclops turned to Conan. "Here. You might like this. The Whites found it laying between two puddles upon the floor of the cavern where you must have been captured by Chuntha." At this statement a shudder seemed to ripple through Wikkell.

"Something wrong?"

Wikkell shook his head. "I suspect I know what those puddles represent. They stir a rather unpleasant memory."

Conan took the sword and did not ask after the source of the cyclops' recollection. The Cimmerian had noted, however, that his ability to hear the mindspeech had left him. He suspected that the cause of that particular talent had somehow been the responsibility of one of the jewels they had stolen from Chuntha, one of those spilled in his hasty escape from her chambers. A pity in one way to have lost it; on the other side of that coin, however, it was magic and apt to cause more trouble in the long run than it was worth. His limited experience with magic had shown Conan that even those who knew how to perform such conjurs often found themselves in difficulties from them, and there were indeed things with which men were not made to tamper.

Conan hefted the solid weight of the sword and smiled at the weapon. Here was something a man could trust and depend upon. A strong arm, cold iron, and skill . . . aye, he would take those over spells any day.

Chuntha awoke from a languorous sleep. She grinned to herself as she stretched . . .

She sat up abruptly, startled. Where was the barbarian? Why did he not lie next to her, dead from his exertions as surely he should be?

Now that she was more awake, Chuntha noted that she did not feel the usual sensation of greatly increased energy that came from having drained a man of his essence. Sated, yes, but empowered, no. What had happened?

She leaped to her feet and strode naked to the chamber's exit. Outside, her guards lay flaccidly in repose upon the cold stone.

"Where is the man? Chuntha's voice, full of anger, cut at the two.

"G-g-gone to f-fetch wh-whatever it w-was you w-wished," the worms replied. "By y-your orders, m-m-mistress, he t-told us—"

"And you let him go? Just like that? Fools! I will see you baking in the lime pits!" She spun away from the stammering worms and stormed back into the chamber. No one had *ever* lain with her and walked away, no one! She had been lax, she had wanted to make him last, that had been her mistake! Well, she would fetch him back and none of his clever manipulations would serve him this time, no matter how pleasant! Conan, he had called himself, was a dead man!

Rey still had a small hope that somehow all this would turn out in his favor. He had, after all, captured three of the loose humans wandering about in his caves, and had melted two others. As nearly as he could tell, only the one, Conan, remained at large. True, the prophesy seemed centered on that man, but even now, half a dozen of his cyclopes marched at top speed to retrieve his quarry. Rey would have gone himself, but he had another foreboding feeling that he was better off for the moment in the seat of his power. Once Conan was returned, the wizard intended to slay all four of the troublemakers quickly and finish the entire unsavory episode. He had thought he might prolong it, taking certain pleasures in the slowness of it, but something about that felt altogether too risky. Puddle them and be done with it, he thought, and get back to business as usual.

Chuntha, even knowing the risk, once again called upon the spell of the metamorphic reptile. She took to the air, rage and shame filling her at hav-

ing lost a game at which she was most expert . . .
to a mere man, and a barbarian at that.

The monster flew, sharp eyes alert, seeking prey.

As Conan and his two new companions moved
through the winding caveways, they found themselves faced suddenly with a half dozen cyclopes.
Upon viewing Conan, the largest of the cyclops,
one who seemed to be the leader, spoke sharply,
obviously an order. The other five cyclopes spread
out and started for Conan.

The Cimmerian drew his sword and prepared to
die. He might cross over into the Gray Lands, but
by Crom, he would not go without taking some of
them with him!

"That will not be needed," Wikkell said, raising
one arm and gesturing at Conan.

The Cimmerian held the sword with both hands,
point aimed at the throat of the nearest approaching cyclops. He did not relax his stance at his
companion's comment.

Wikkell stepped forward and called out to the
leader of the cyclopes, speaking in a harsh and
choppy language that Conan did not understand.
The leader replied, and a short exchange of dia-
logue followed, at the end of which the leader
ordered his troops to stop.

Conan raised slightly from his bent-kneed fighting stance and lowered the point of his blade.
"What did you say to them?"

"I told them there was about to be a revolution
against the witch and the wizard. Anyone who
stood against the action would certainly die for it,
as would anyone who tampered with my short

friend with the sword here—that is to say, you. Jalouri, the leader of Rey's guards over there, informs me that his loyalties to the wizard have never really been all that solid, and he has indicated that he and his troops would be more than happy to assist us in any way they can."

"Good of him," Conan said.

"One does not need to be a fish to know which way the tide flows," Wikkell said.

Conan sheathed his sword. "Lead on, friend."

The party, now swelled by six, moved on.

"I think I might be able to slip my hands out of these manacles," Elashi said. "They are very loose upon my wrists."

"A stupid idea," Lalo said. "Neither Tull nor I can do so, and what good would it do you to be free? Do you think you can bypass the wizard and his guards?"

"Perhaps not," Elashi said, irritated, "but there might be something in this chamber I can use to free you. At the very least we might be able to strike the wizard down, can we find a weapon."

"Her idea has merit," Tull said. "I'd rather take a few of 'em with me, do I have to leave this life."

Lalo merely shrugged and looked dubious. One of his smaller insults.

Elashi strained and tugged at the cuff on her right wrist. The skin peeled back next to the rusty metal and blood flowed, lubricating her hand. The two men watched as she managed to pull her hand loose. The left hand came free easier, since she had the right to help, but blood also oozed from scrapes there when she was done. Her wrists hurt, but not so much as all that, especially considering what the alternative would shortly be.

Quietly, and with great care, she stole across the chamber toward a large trunk against the far wall. Perhaps there would be something inside it she could use.

She wondered about Conan. Had he met his end at the teeth of the monster that had snatched him into the air? She hoped not; for all of his faults, Elashi had grown to like Conan more than a little. Of course he was not so witty as Lalo, who despite his curse, seemed a most clever companion. Still, she would not like to think of Conan dead. They had gone through much together, and he was so young. It would be such a waste.

Do not worry about that now, Elashi, she told herself. Whatever has happened to Conan, you must try to keep yourself alive.

She hurried over to the chest.

Twenty-four

In the largest chamber he had yet seen, Conan observed from a high ledge thousands of occupants: worms, cyclopes, Bloodbats, and Whites, mostly keeping together in like groups, but here and there a few mingling without regard for kind. A low rumble of conversation filled the cave as the thousands below talked among themselves.

Wikkell and Deek moved to the edge of the shelf, and the cyclops took a deep breath and yelled at the assemblage:

"Ho, brothers! Listen to me!"

The drone of speech faded to silence as those below looked up at Wikkell. There was a long pause, filled with anticipation, before the cyclops spoke again.

"The time has come for us to restore our world to what it once was," he said. His voice boomed out loudly, carrying to all parts of the chamber. "Those who have held us in thrall for so long must be removed, forever!"

A loud cheer broke from the crowd, hoots and yells and high-pitched whistles. He definitely had their attention.

"Your leaders will tell you of your duties. The witch and the wizard will not relinquish their control easily, and they are powerful, but the time has come!"

Another wave of approbation swelled from the ranks, louder than before. Wikkell turned away.

"G-g-good sp-speech," Deek said.

"I hope it was not my last one," Wikkell said. He glanced at the barbarian. "Ready?"

Conan nodded. "Aye." He grinned. Here was a situation he could enjoy: battle, with no complexity to it.

The Whites would attack the sanctums of both witch and wizard simultaneously, followed by the bats, then a mix of worm and cyclopian troops. The bats would also fly back and forth, reporting messages as needed. Somewhere in the midst of all that, Conan would seek to find and free his friends. It was simple enough. His favorite kind of plan. It might fail, but at least it would not do so due to some serpentine twist that went awry.

Conan led Wikkell and Deek down the path toward Katamay Rey's cave.

Elashi rummaged around in the trunk, discarding items that offered no apparent use to her. She found a stoppered vial and turned to show it to Lalo and Tull.

"Should I open this?"

"Better you should not," Lalo said. "We do not know what resides within, and it might be something we would rather not know intimately."

Elashi nodded and tossed the vial into a pile of clothing already pulled from the trunk.

Further searching produced a rod of shining metal. The thing was the diameter of Elashi's little finger and as long as the distance between her thumb tip and forefinger. There was a knobby protrusion near one end. Curious as to the object's function, Elashi pressed the knob. Fortunately, the opposite end was not pointed at any part of herself; rather, the tip of the rod was aimed at the pile of clothes next to the trunk. A bright and jagged white light erupted from the rod with a crackling noise like that of a large fire, and the pile of clothing sizzled and burst into flame.

Elashi dropped the rod. "Mitra!"

"Best stay away from that, girl," Tull said.

"No, fool," Lalo said. "Bring it here."

"You want me to touch that again? What if it discharges another of those lightninglike bolts?"

"I hope that it does," Lalo said. "At the chains that bind us. Where is your wit, woman? And hurry, in case the wizard has heard the noise and comes to investigate!"

With the clothing burning and filling the chamber with flickering orange light, Elashi picked up the magical rod and scurried back toward Lalo and Tull.

                    *   *   *

In the guise of the flying reptile, Chuntha soared high around a wide turning in one of the major tunnels, and beheld a most surprising sight: below was a collection of Blind Whites, hurrying along the corridor. Behind the Whites and not much above them, a flock of Bloodbats flitted along.

What misdeed was this? Whites and bats, intent on some purpose, and together?

Chuntha puzzled over the event, heretofore unseen.

There was more: behind the first two groups, at some distance, came a gathering of giant worms and cyclopes! Hundreds of them, moving along as if they had been born of the same mothers instead of enemies for scores upon scores of years.

Oh, dear.

Whatever the cause of this phenomenon, Chuntha immediately knew that such a collaboration of the cave's inhabitants was *not* to her advantage. In fact, she reasoned that it could mean nothing but disaster. The only place they could be going was her chambers, and from the look of them, they did not intend to fall down and worship her when they arrived.

Sensha's damnation! That prophesy of unnamed disaster had come forth despite all of her efforts to thwart it!

Given her present circumstances, wrapped within a spell whose longevity could not be depended upon, Chuntha had no desire to see if the weight of her magic could prevail against such an unruly looking mob as that below her. Besides, most of her magical apparati lay back at her chambers.

Had Rey done this? No, she thought, likely not.

Conan had somehow engineered it, as the prophesy had hinted he would. Frightening, to think that a man without any apparent sorcery about him could cause such things. Not only had he resisted her carnal magics, but now this.

The mark of a wise witch was the knowledge of when to stay and when to leave, and no doubt about it, it was time to move on. Better she should forget about Conan, the wizard, the caves, and everything connected with them. Chuntha was not fond of the idea of losing, but she was less fond of the idea of dying.

Unseen by those below, the magical creature flew on with increased speed.

Elashi pointed the end of the rod at the chains holding Lalo to the wall. She closed her eyes and pressed the stud.

Nothing happened.

The desert woman opened her eyes. She pressed the knob again. A kind of thin whine came from the rod.

"So much for that idea," Tull said. "Looks like it only had one bolt in it."

"Maybe not," Lalo said. "Maybe it just needs to gather more magic for a time. Wait for a few moments and try again . . . unless you have pressing matters elsewhere to which you must attend?"

After a short wait, Elashi again pointed the rod at Lalo's chains and touched the knob. She expected nothing, but Lalo's surmise proved correct: a bright bolt zapped forth and struck the iron links. Elashi again dropped the device, but the force of the magic had already done its job. The chains binding Lalo to the wall ring had shattered under the impact of the blinding energy.

"The wizard must be deaf," Tull said as Lalo moved to retrieve the magic rod.

"Perhaps he is out," Lalo said, "looking for flies from which to pull the wings." He picked up the rod and examined it. "Patience, Tull old fool. We shall have you free in a few moments."

Lalo waited for what he considered an appropriate length of time before he tried the device again. True to his words, the thing functioned as it had twice before, and Tull's chains fell away. They were free!

Rey had been sleeping soundly, but even so, the use of potent magic so near had roused him. He felt rather than heard it, and swam up from slumber. The first thing he noticed was the smell of burning cloth. What had caused that? Fire was mostly a stranger to the caves, since virtually everything in them was too damp to burn without difficulty. But that was definitely the stench of scorched wool, and very near.

The captives. They must have done something they should not have been able to do.

Rey sighed. He could not even gather a few minutes of sleep without being interrupted. Enough of this. He had planned to keep them alive, to guarantee the capture of their comrade, Conan, but not if it meant he had to suffer for it. He would kill them now and take his chances on the barbarian's recovery.

Rey arose from his bed and went to the chamber where he had left the prisoners.

He very nearly ran into them.

The three of them had somehow managed to get free of their chains! They were but a few spans from him as he entered the chamber, and apparently hurrying to leave. He raised his hands in a curse-casting posture.

"Stop where you stand!" he ordered.

One of them, the cursed grinning man, extended something in Rey's direction. The wizard immediately recognized it as his lightning rod. If it had sufficient charge to send a bolt, he could be in trouble.

"Hot!" Rey yelled, waggling his fingers.

The grinning man yelped and dropped the rod, now a glowing orange from the small spell Rey had cast upon it.

"You have caused me enough trouble," Rey said. "I am about to be shut of you. Give my regards to the damned souls in Gehanna."

But as he raised his hands again to melt the three, a noise intruded on his concentration. It sounded as if someone was approaching the entrance to his chambers from the main corridor. A lot of someones, actually. Could it be his cyclopes, returning with Conan already? No, it was too soon. Who, then?

The noise grew quite loud. A kind of droning chant.

Best he go see what it was; the two guards out front could not be trusted to handle anything more complex than feeding themselves and defecating.

"Stay here!" Rey commanded. "Move through this portal and you will certainly regret it."

With that, Rey turned to go see what all the noise was about.

Chuntha knew of several ways to the surface. She regretted that she would not be able to return to her chambers to retrieve certain of her favorite possessions, but she also considered herself lucky to have made her escape so easily. True, she could have withstood a lengthy attack provided she had been able to see it coming in time; doubtless she could have slain a goodly number of the revolutionaries in the process as well. Then again, it did not matter if she killed hundreds of them if, in the end, they managed to overcome her.

Soaring along, praying to assorted dark deities that the spell would hold until she could make good her escape, Chuntha could not help but feel curious as to just how Conan had inspired this revolt.

One of the hidden exits to the world above lay not far from the wizard's quarters. It was, in fact, the closest of such egresses, and the witch felt she might chance it in her present form. Why not? It would warm her black soul to see if the wizard had troubles as bad as her own.

The reptile that was also a witch altered its course when it came to a wide bifurcation in the large tunnel.

Katamay Rey reached his chambers' entrance and looked out.

What the wizard saw filled him with utter surprise and shock: a horde of Blind Whites advanced toward him, and behind them, a flock of Bloodbats darkened the air with their numbers.

By Set's scaled scrotum! What was this?

The two guards normally posted were nowhere to be seen.

Rey ducked back inside, feeling a moment of panic. He had not survived all these centuries by being entirely stupid. He was about to come under attack, and if he wanted to live to see more centuries, he had best do something, and quickly!

Over the years he had perhaps grown a bit arrogant, he realized. Hundreds of years past, when first he had arrived at the caves, the wizard had been more cautious. He had set traps to protect himself in the event of just such an attack, but in the ensuing decades and centuries, he had almost forgotten about his protections. Many had fallen into disrepair or, in the case of those involving magic, lost their potency. But there remained one he had never deactivated.

Rey hurriedly rehearsed the words of the old spell, trying to be certain he recalled them correctly. He stepped back out into the hallway and faced the oncoming horde. The Whites could not see per se, but they were aware of him through their augmented senses of hearing and smell.

They charged, full tilt, screaming. The bats flew right behind the wave of running Whites.

Rey spoke aloud the words of the ancient spell, gesturing at the ceiling of the corridor as he did so.

Suddenly the tunnel was filled with the roar of uncounted tons of rock breaking loose from the age-old ceiling. The noise of the avalanche was

followed immediately by the screams of those below. The roof did not entirely collapse, nor did the
rocks that fell do so all at once, but the position of
the attackers made it quite impossible for them to
escape the cascade of rocks that showered down
upon them. Despite the dampness, dust and grit
flew. Moans arose from the shattered victims, those
still capable of mounting speech. Red splashed
and coated the walls. It was a hard rain indeed.

When the last rock dropped, what remained was
a corridor now somewhat shallower on the bottom
and deeper at the top than before. The new floor
was that much higher for the bodies under the
former ceiling. Two or three Whites had avoided
the trap, and several bats flew around in dazed
circles, but the attack was broken.

Rey grinned, pleased with himself . . . until he
saw the first rank of worms and cyclopes begin
climbing over the rockfall. Set and all the demi-
demons!

Twenty-five

The fire that had burned the pile of clothing had begun to die down when from it there came a *pop*!

Elashi, Lalo, and Tull all turned at the sudden sound and stared at the fading light of the smoldering clothing.

"What was that?" Tull asked.

Elashi shook her head.

Lalo said, "That vial you tossed into the clothing. I think perhaps the fire has opened it."

No sooner had Lalo said this than a poisonous-looking black vapor arose from the dying fire. The tendrils of black appeared to be unaffected by the fire's heat—and it looked nothing at all like normal smoke. As the three watched, the curling black swirled up and began to move toward them, pulsing as if to some unheard rhythm.

"Uh-oh," Tull said. "I like the look of this not at all."

"What can we do?" The wizard has threatened to blast us if we move from this chamber," Elashi said.

"Better the demon we know than one we do not," Lalo told her, nodding at the malignant vapor undulating slowly toward them. "Besides, it sounds to me as if the wizard might have his hands occupied at the moment."

Neither Tull nor Elashi chose to argue with Lalo's assessment of the situation. The black cloud was growing in size; already it blotted out half of the chamber.

The three scrambled for the doorway.

Conan moved along the corridor next to Wikkell and Deek. Ahead, the ceiling had just fallen in with a sound like constant thunder, burying the advance ranks of Whites and bats. The wizard was not without his defenses, so it seemed. The Cimmerian sheathed his sword in order to better clamber over the uneven piles of rock now blanketing the floor.

The witch who was a flying reptile approached the scene of carnage and flapped down to perch on a shelf high above it all. My, my. That Bastard most assuredly had his problems. Could the magicked beast have performed the action, it would have grinned. Chuntha decided that she could tarry here for a bit and watch. It seemed that the wizard was finally about to get his just due, and this was too good a show to miss.

Rey's skills had fallen into disuse over the years, but there had been a time when he was as adept a spellcaster as any. He dredged up old curses and conjurations from his long past, searching for one that would put a decisive end to this attack. There was a demon-call he had used once, oh, three or four hundred years ago. As he recalled, the demon had been both large and fearsome, with a hideous visage. Yes, he would set the demon upon the blasted worms and traitorous cyclopes and see how they enjoyed that!

Could he but recall the words of the damned spell in time . . .

Tull, Elashi, and Lalo ran into the antechamber and skidded to a halt. The wizard was not to be seen.

"Outside, he must be outside, in the corridor," Elashi said, pointing at the door.

"We cannot go out there," Tull said.

"Well, no doubt the black vapor behind us will stop at the open doorway through which we have just passed," Lalo said, his voice heavy with irony.

Elashi shook her head. Lalo was right. What were they going to do?

Chuntha's observation post gave her a good view of the proceedings below; That Bastard, give him credit, had more than a few things left up his sleeve. The witch watched with respect as the air began to swirl inside the hastily sketched pentagram on the floor in front of the entrance to the wizard's chambers. Calling up something, he was, and she doubted that such an act would do the attacking rebels any good whatsoever.

Wait—what was that?—no, *who* was that? Conan! Climbing over the fallen rock, in company with the cyclopes and worms.

For a moment Chuntha's rage was such that she nearly took to the air, intending to dive down and rend the cursed barbarian into tattered and bloody flesh. But no. Wait a moment and see what the wizard works, she thought. No point in being foolish.

The reason Rey had chosen the location of his chambers originally from all the thousands available was simple enough: the magic permeating the old rock here hung thick and potent. A spell that might exhaust some other location might hardly take a small fraction of the energies resident in this particular area. So it was that the wizard had sufficient force to conjure the demon.

Within the bounds of the pentagram, the air twirled and became a flashing display of purple and yellow, much like a liquid bruise upon the atmosphere. Came a loud clap of noise and suddenly the demon, one of Set's lesser messengers, named Tunk, appeared in an eye-smiting flare of light. Tunk was easily twice the size of the largest cyclops, thrice the weight in his earthly form, and bristling with dagger-sized black claws on hands and feet. His mouth—and there was no doubt of his maleness to anyone with even the smallest of vision—his mouth opened in a grimace that became a roar. Teeth like a boar's tusks flashed in the light of Tunk's arrival, and the sound he made might be likened to that of iron plates banged and scraped together with great force.

Tunk's appearance put a halt to the advancing horde of worms and cyclopes as quickly as if those worthies had reached the end of a stout tether.

"Go and kill them, all of them!" Rey ordered. "I call upon you with your true name Tunk, and demand that you obey."

Tunk, of course, had no choice; still, his rage at being jerked away from a most interesting encounter with a demoness in Gehanna was such that killing something would have come easily enough without an order. The demon leaped from the pentagram toward the startled worms and cyclopes.

Wikkell sucked in a deep breath as he saw the monstrous apparition bound from where it appeared in front of the wizard. It was coming right at him, it seemed, and the small form of Conan perched atop a new-made hill in between did little to give the cyclops confidence that he would survive for long once that *thing* arrived. Panic flowed through Wikkell, and he scrabbled in his belt for a weapon, any weapon, he might use to defend himself.

Conan must have been as startled and frightened as he, the cyclops thought, and yet the man, less than a third the size of the onrushing demon, drew his sword and raised it.

Amazing, that this puny human would dare to stand with what amounted to a small sliver of iron against such a behemoth. Doomed, and yet standing his ground Conan was, and no one could see such a thing and not feel admiration against the amazement that anyone could be so foolish as to hope to prevail.

The thing reached the base of the rocky slope upon which Conan stood and began its ascent.

The problem was that after it crushed Conan, Wikkell and Deek were next in line.

The black vapor lapped at the edges of the inner chamber's doorway behind the three people, then slowly began to ooze across the floor like some cold and thick liquid.

Tull, Elashi, and Lalo moved across the antechamber away from the blackness, toward the exit. Now they could see the wizard outside, directing some hellish monster's attack against a gathering of worms and cyclopes and—yes!—Conan!

Not that he had a chance against the thing that rushed toward him. The giant beast made Conan look tiny, perched as he was atop a hill of rock, sword raised. The monster screamed in a roaring gong of a voice as it charged.

Rey smiled in triumph. Best *this*, fools! he thought as Tunk sprinted toward Conan and his doomed friends.

Chuntha watched, trying to remain detached, she could not help feeling the excitement as the demon prepared to destroy Conan and the rebels. This would be most bloody . . . and most amusing.

*　　*　　*

"D-d-do s-s-something!" Deek scraped.

Wikkell came up with the graystone jar full of pale powder they had stolen from the wizard's chambers. No good—wait! Perhaps it might help.

Instantly Wikkell saw that he would have but one chance, and that one slim. The timing must be perfect; a mistake would be instantly fatal. Then again, it was not as if there were a number of choices left to him. Better a small chance than none at all.

"Conan!" Wikkell yelled. "When I yell again, leap to the side!"

"What?" Conan did not turn, but kept his gaze upon the thing bounding up the side of the hill at him.

"Just do it! I have a plan!"

Conan considered his options. He might inflict a nasty wound upon that *thing* coming at him, but he had little hope of slaying it outright before it swiped at him with one of those clawed hands or feet and disemboweled him. If Wikkell had a plan, Conan was not averse to trying it. He could always die swinging his blade later, if it came to that.

"Aye!" Conan yelled. He bent his knees further.

Rey watched as his enthralled demon sprang up the hillside. Another leap and he would be upon Conan, and good riddance—!

"Now, Conan, now!" the cyclops behind the Cimmerian yelled.

Was not that Wikkell, his old assistant? Rey wondered. I thought him dead . . .

As he watched, Conan leaped agilely to one side,

tumbling and falling on the loose rock as he landed, out of the demon's path. Well, no matter. Tunk could attend to Conan after he slew the cyclopes and the worms.

Wikkell swung his arm, as if casting something. What was he doing? Rey could not see anything, no . . . wait, something glittered in the green light, some kind of dust.

The cyclops leaped to one side and the worm next to him slithered the opposite way just as Tunk landed on the spot where Conan had only recently been.

Tunk's feet shot out from under him and he fell upon his back, hard. As heavy as Tunk was, he should have hit the rock and stuck, but instead, he skipped over the ground as a cast stone does over water—once, twice—and on the second bounce, flew into the air a good span high. The demon sailed like a bird for a moment; unfortunately for him, Tunk was not a creature of the air in his current form, and his flight became less birdlike and more like a boulder.

The demon hit the ground past the base of the slope after having gone perhaps fifty paces through the air, dropping an easy four spans.

Rey felt the earth shake beneath him when Tunk slammed into the cave's floor. Such a fall would have killed any man who ever lived, and most likely anything else born of nature as well. Even a demon could not withstand such an impact without damage, as long as he wore solid flesh.

But Tunk *was* a demon, and while his recovery would have been painful, he would have risen from the fall in a moment or two, shaken but more enraged than ever, except that the force of the impact shook loose a few of the more solidly entrenched roof rocks that had resisted the wizard's earlier release spell.

Two house-sized boulders fell. The first landed squarely upon Tunk's prone form, driving him into the rock as a man drives a tent peg with a large mallet.

The second boulder, somewhat larger than the first, came down upon the big rock, and thus drove it into the floor, shattering the top of the first and the bottom of the second. What was thus formed looked much like a rather fat mushroom when the dust settled.

There were limits even to a demon's power, Rey knew. Tunk was not going to be digging out from under that any time soon, if ever.

The wizard looked and saw Conan rising to his feet, sword in hand. Best to retreat to his chambers, Rey thought, to consider his next move. And now!

The black miasma had swirled to fill nearly all of the antechamber. Elashi, Tull, and Lalo crouched at the doorway watching the darkness come toward them. Lalo said, "We have to get out of here, at once!"

With that, the three of them turned and sprang for the exit—just as the wizard leaped at the portal from the other side. The four collided and fell sprawling.

Fortunately for the three captives, their combined weight was enough to force the fall to end outside the chambers. As they tried to untangle themselves, they heard a screech of something whose voice they recognized: the flying reptile that had taken Conan before.

Chuntha could stand it no longer. The wizard, That stupid Bastard! had failed to kill Conan and stop the attack. His enthralled demon lay flattened under solid rock, and Conan—that vile, wretched, beautiful barbarian—was still alive.

It was too much. The only man to ever shame her in bed must die, that was the beginning and end of it. The witch leaped into the air and flapped downward in a flight she intended to end with her claws buried in Conan's heart.

Screeching in primal rage, the reptile dived . . .

Conan ran toward his three friends and the fallen wizard. Ten paces, five, he would be upon them in an instant, and his sword would claim the wizard's head, by Crom! He raised the blade to strike—

The screech from above called Conan's attention. He looked up to see the ensorceled witch coming through the air at him. He immediately saw that he would not be able to reach the wizard before the flying reptile would intercept him. He turned toward the witch. A lucky strike might take a wing, he thought, though it was much more likely that the toothed snout would take him first. Well, he would met his end as a man, sword swinging. He twisted to face the new threat.

I have you now! Chuntha thought. Prepare to die, Conan!

She was five armspans from Conan and dropping fast when the spell enshrouding the true form of the witch failed.

One moment she was a terrible and ferocious thing from the early dawn of life on earth; the next moment the leathery form vanished. Chuntha screamed, and the voice was that of a woman.

Conan saw the change, as quick as an eyeblink. What was a scaled monster became a naked woman, hair streaming back in the wind of her flight, now a fall heading straight at him. The Cimmerian was startled; not so much that he failed to leap lithely out of the witch's path, but enough so that he did not swing the sword to slash at her.

The sword was not necessary in the end, however.

Chuntha the witch hit the rock floor with less force than had Rey's demon, but it was more than sufficient enough to end her days on earth. She bounced only once, stopped. The naked form seemed almost unmarked on the back, but the face and front had become red jelly and splintered white bone in an instant.

As Conan watched, the smooth beauty of the witch's back and buttocks and legs shriveled, as quick as a dry leaf cast into a hot fire. In an instant, nothing but black ash remained of the form that had been kept alive for long years past the day when it should have died.

Chuntha the witch was no more.

Conan turned back toward the wizard. He was still alive, and did Conan not attend to that, the evil sorcerer might do to him what Chuntha had just done to herself.

Lalo and Tull were helping Elashi to crawl away from the chamber's entrance when the wizard managed to attain his feet. He looked at the approaching Conan, shook his head, and turned toward the portal. He leaped inside.

Conan rushed after the wizard. Best to stop him before he could mount another magical attack.

"Conan, no!" Elashi screamed. "Do not go in there!"

The Cimmerian was but a few steps away from the entrance and moving fast when he heard Elashi's yell. Something in her voice warned him of great danger, and he managed to alter his path. He skidded and slid, and dropped his sword. He had to put both hands out to keep from smashing head-on into the wall next to the entrance. As he did this, he heard the wizard cry out, a high-pitched and terrible sound. Something had him.

What ungodly thing lay within?

A moment later Katamay Rey stepped out, stumbling past Conan.

The Cimmerian could not be certain it *was* the wizard at first. The creature who staggered past him was wrapped in black flame that seemed to consume him. Flesh crackled like fat dropped into a heated skillet, and the man's screams were continuous.

Conan retrieved his fallen sword and started toward the man. Slaying him would surely be a mercy, though that was not Conan's motivation.

He raised the sword.

Rey knew he was dying. There was no cure for the Black Rot; it would burn him to nothingness

in a matter of moments. Not even the most powerful healing spell he knew would delay it for a second.

Through his pain and rage, Rey accepted his
end. He would die, there was no help for it. But,
by Set, he would take all those around him to
Gehanna with him!

Even a dying wizard has power, and wizards do
not die easily or fast, even under decay of Black
Rot. He would have time to kill them all and bring
the cave down around their ears!

With his final conscious thoughts, Rey unleashed
all the powers at his command. Not stopped, such
energies would consume everything for half a day's
walk in all directions.

Conan stopped in mid-stride, blade lifted to strike;
as if he had hit wall of packed feathers, or encoun-
tered one of the fierce winter winds of his home-
land, a wind a big man could lean into without
falling. He could force himself forward a little but
then it pushed back at him, this invisible barrier.
What—?

The wizard began to glow under the black flame.
Rays of red and yellow and blue light shot forth,
lighting the dim cave to the brightness of full day-
light, albeit a day like none ever seen by mortal
man.

Rocks rumbled and seemed to leap up and fly
away from the ground around the tortured form of
the wizard.

A weird humming—like the wings of a million
bees—began.

Conan felt a weakness enter him, turning his

arms and legs into pigs of lead. He wanted nothing so much as to lie down, to rest . . .

A crackling beam shot out from the wizard's face, or where Conan assumed the face had been, and the beam lanced into one of the cyclops half-way across the corridor. The cyclops exploded, bursting into thousands of pieces, shattering like glass.

Around Conan the air seemed suddenly filled with ice, so cold was it all of a moment, and yet a second later the air seemed as hot as if it were from an oven. Then the heat faded . . . and still Conan could not move.

The Cimmerian realized the great threat. The wizard, whatever his condition, was still danger-ous. He had to strike him down—or they might all die.

Against the force of the invisible barrier, Conan strived to move. An inch, two, three he managed, only to be pushed back past his starting place. And he felt wearier with each passing second. If he could but rest, for only a moment, he could finish this . . .

No! Conan told himself. Any rest now would likely be his last.

The humming increased; the rays grew brighter, turning the wizard into something that could not be gazed upon without going blind; and the crack-ling beams shot forth and blasted at the cyclopes and the worms. One of the beams barely missed Conan; he felt the heat of its passing. The ceiling rumbled overhead, as did the walls and the floor.

Conan closed his eyes. Even through their lids he could see the bright glow that the wizard had become. He pushed again against the unseen barrier, utilizing his great strength to its utmost. The Cimmerian youth managed to lower the blade, knowing he could not swing it in a cut. He pushed against the wall of feathers, leaned into the magic wind, gaining a step, then two, the muscles of his legs bulging with the effort, the sinews creaking with the strain.

Rocks fell from the ceiling, but Conan ignored them. Another step, a tiny one, like a small child might take. His boots slid backward a hair on the stone, but he willed himself forward, pressing down as well as forward, gripping the ground through the leather of his shod feet as best he could.

A section of wall collapsed behind Conan, followed by more rock from the ceiling. He felt the floor shudder and shift under him. Another moment or two of this and an earthquake would likely bury them all.

But try as he might, Conan could get no closer. The point of his blade was only a handspan away from the shining wizard, but it might as well have been a thousand miles.

Then, over the unnatural noises produced by the dying wizard, there came a single voice, cutting as only it could through the cacophony, the voice of Lalo, the cursed one:

"I knew he could not do it! Such a weakling!"

Conan's rage could no longer be contained. All of Lalo's previous insults added to his ire, and this one was the final straw. Weakling? Weakling! I will show you who is a weakling!

Burning with the fires of outrage and insult, Conan bunched his powerful thews in a final, total effort. He lunged, slowly for all his strength, but a definite surge forward.

The point of Conan's blued-iron sword touched the rotting form of the wizard on the chest over his black heart, paused for the briefest of instants, then plunged through and sliced open the throbbing pump. Blood sprayed forth in a fountain, covering Conan.

After what seemed like forever, the wizard collapsed.

The lights winked out, the humming stopped cold, the walls and ceiling stilled.

The silence after Rey's fall was almost tangible.

Then the quiet was broken. Without a trace of irony in his voice, Lalo said quietly, "Well, I stand corrected."

Nobody had anything to say for quite a while after that.

Twenty~six

Wikkell and Deek moved to where the remains of the wizard lay on the rock and stared at the spot. A thin black powder covered the floor there, all that was left of the once-powerful mage.

Several more of the cyclopes and worms moved in to look upon the dust and ash that had been wizard and witch.

"We have won," Wikkell said.

"I-i-indeed."

Some of the cyclopes approached Wikkell, and a contingent of worms moved with them.

What, they asked, do we do now?

As easily as that, Wikkell and Deek found themselves cast in the role of rulers.

*   *   *

Conan sheathed his sword and went to his friends.

Lalo had arisen and moved to stare into the wizard's chambers. "The black smoke is gone," he said. "And the wizard and the witch are both dead, thanks to you, Conan. You are most resourceful."

The Cimmerian shook his head. Could his ears be deceiving him? Had Lalo offered a compliment without a cutting edge? He waited for the verbal slash, but none came. And when Lalo turned to look at the others, something even more amazing occurred:

Lalo had stopped smiling.

Elashi spoke first. "Lalo! Your face!"

Lalo reached up to touch his mouth. The smile returned, but it was different this time. "The curse! It . . . it is *gone!*"

Elashi ran to Lalo and embraced him.

Tull and Conan glanced at each other. Tull said, "The wizard's dying must have done it."

Conan nodded. He looked on as Lalo and Elashi hugged, but he felt no sense of jealousy. They seemed destined for each other, and his path was to have diverged from that of the desert woman's soon in any event.

Lalo and Elashi broke their embrace and turned to regard Conan. Each looked abashed.

Conan grinned. "Nay," he said. "You two shall have my blessing." To himself, Conan thought: although you might come to see this as a curse someday too, Lalo; her tongue is as sharp as yours was, and without any spell to drive it.

Wikkell and Deek approached the Cimmerian. The cyclops smiled. "We owe you much, Conan," he said. "Without you, we would still be enslaved. How can we repay you?"

That question needed no contemplation whatsoever. "Show us the way out of here," Conan said.

"D-d-done," the worm said.

So it was that Conan, Tull, Elashi, and Lalo were taken along a twisted corridor that wound upward. Against the dim green of the glow-fungus, a shaft of almost solid-looking white light stabbed down at the end of the tunnel: sunshine, from the world above.

"There," Wikkell said. "There is the entrance to your world."

Conan nodded and extended his right hand. Wikkell understood the gesture, and his own huge hand enveloped the Cimmerian's hand in a powerful squeeze. The two smiled at each other. "Go in peace, Conan."

"F-f-farewell," Deek added.

Tull, Elashi, and Lalo had already hurried up the incline and out of the cave when Conan turned away from the worm and the cyclops and walked toward the exit. In his belt pouch he still had a handful of valuable gems, which he would divide equally with the others. Not enough to make any of them rich, but enough to keep them in food and drink for some time. And they had come through the duel with witch and wizard exhausted, but alive and unharmed. It could have been much worse, but never had he been so glad to see the end of an adventure.

Striding boldly, Conan of Cimmeria walked into

the sunshine and out of the dim caves. He blinked against the unaccustomed brightness of the day.

A few spans away his friends awaited him, but for the moment Conan was content to stand with the warmth of the sun on his face and the cold wind ruffling his dark hair. Free! At last!

Then he smiled and walked away from the entrance to the vast caves. He did not look back.